A Boss'd Up Holiday With The Plug 2

PREVIOUSLY IN A BOSSED UP HOLIDAY WITH THE PLUG...

SOMETHING NEW

Kia

After seeing Nadia in the mall, I was lost as to why she didn't speak to me. When Yams spoke to her, I knew this nigga was a dope pusher. Even though he tried to play it smooth, I knew when a nigga was talking in code. The rest of the evening, I was side eying him, because I wanted to know why front like you're a legitimate businessman, when you knew you weren't. When Yams pulled up in my driveway and helped me get my shopping bags inside the house, he stood by the door, as I walked from the kitchen and stood in front of him.

"So, look, I'm real smart Zeke. Tell me the truth. You push dope?" I asked him straight up. He stared in my eyes as if he was reading me. He showed no emotion, as we stood in silence.

"Listen, I do own several legitimate businesses. I'm not sure what gave you the idea otherwise."

"Look just tell me the truth. Like give me the opportunity to make decisions for myself," I pleaded with him. I really liked Zeke. He was refreshing, and we had been honest to each other up until now. I was looking for someone that was legit, that way I could do the same. I was tired of the hustling. I was tired of feeling like I needed to look over my shoulder. He stared at me and was just about to say something when, I heard a knock at my door. I walked around him and went to the door. I saw a tall white burly man through the window. The man looked so familiar, but I couldn't figure out where I saw him at. He carried himself like a bodyguard and he had a black bag in his hand. It looked just like the bag Renzo would use to bring me money. At that point, I opened the door and he handed me the bag.

"There is a message for you in the bag," he stated and walked away. I was so damn confused. The bag was heavy. I turned around and the look Yams gave me, I knew I had to explain what the hell just happened, but I was confused myself. I closed the door and walked over to the kitchen island and sat the bag down without looking in it.

"What was that about?" he asked curiously.

"I think my cousin had them drop this bag over, but back to what we were discussing?" I changed the subject, but I knew Yams was a very inquisitive person and would definitely revisit this question.

"Let me ask you something. Are you being honest with me? You're questioning my honesty, but you definitely got some red flags, shawty." He spoke his truth as he leaned on the counter, and eyed the black bag. I knew I wanted a different type of relationship and ever since I left from out of town, I had been spending all my time with Yams. I enjoyed the date nights, and him being so attentive to me. So, I decided to be straight forward with him.

"Look, you got some where to go?" I asked him and he shook his head no. "I will be upfront with you as long as you keep it gangsta with me," I truthfully told him. I grabbed him by the hand and pulled him towards the living room. I made him sit on the couch and I sat right next to him. I was just about to tell him what I did to make money when I heard a banging at my door.

"Well who the fuck is that?" I said out loud. I got up and headed to the door seeing a panicked Amber. "Girl, what's wrong with you!" I shouted.

"Kia, OMG we are caught. Kia he took my laptop," Amber rambled on, over and over. She was flushed and looked very stressed.

"The fuck you mean?" I looked at her as if she was crazy. I looked around her to see if Yams was listening, but I noticed he was in his phone. I grabbed Amber by the arm, taking her down the hall.

"Get your shit together and tell me what the fuck is going on?" I harshly whispered. She took a deep breath and looked at me and then down the hall.

"Wait a minute. Is that Yams?" Amber asked. Just like her to stop what she needed to say to be fucking nosey. She came in here hyperventilating and shit, but now she calm and being nosey.

"Girl, say what you need to say. What were you rambling about when you came through the door?" I questioned her, trying to rush her so she could leave.

"Mack took the laptop. He got the laptop and when I went in my damn purse, the USB drive is gone too," she panicked. I knew her silly ass was going to regret those cameras in the house, and I told her dumb ass to get rid of the USB drive. I shook my head at my cousin because she was being so careless, but something in her eyes that screamed there was more to this story.

"Amber, there is more to this story. What the hell you not telling me?" I asked her.

"I had Troy in the house," she blurted out and I pulled her further down the hall trying to shush her silly ass.

"So, your dumb ass had another nigga in the house, that you put cameras in to watch Mack's ass? Girl this has got to be a joke," I began to laugh, but the seriousness in her voice told it all. "I can't bail you out of this, there is no telling where Mack is. I got my own shit to deal with. I mean was the dick good at least?" I asked her because I needed to know was this extra trouble she had got herself into was even worth it.

"Bitch I didn't even get the dick. I kicked him out as soon as we kissed," she whined. I felt bad for my cousin because on top of all the deception, Mack was about to find out this nigga was in his home. He was about to see cameras of Amber being disloyal and he left Tina for that shit.

"Amber, I can't deal with your shit and my own shit," I looked at Amber and the tears began to fall. I felt so bad for my cousin, but this was the karma for what she did to Tina. They say how you

9

got him, is how you lose them and that was a true damn fact. "Listen, go in the room. I'm going to get rid of Yams." I told her, and she nodded her head in agreement. Walking back out to Yams, he was patiently waiting in his phone.

"Hey, Yams can we pick up where we left off later tonight?" I asked him. He nodded his head, got up and walked over to me. He wrapped his arms around me and hugged me, pulling me closer for a deep kiss. This wasn't our first rodeo when it came to kisses.

"So, when I come back, you going to let me give you some more kisses where you like it right?" He more so was letting me know then demanding me. My cheeks turned a rose red as I blushed hard thinking about our first time we were sexual. I nodded my head yes as I bit my bottom lip. He leaned down to kiss me again. The door opening never broke our kiss. It was hearing Renzo's voice that made me jump.

"The fuck!" he snapped. The look in Renzo's eyes made me want to hide. As he stood there mugging the hell out of me and Yams, I heard Amber's footsteps. As we all looked down the hall, Amber never looked up as she looked in her hand at the stick she was holding. All the color drained from my body as I faced her.

"Kia! Am I reading this shit right? It says... Oh shit!" Amber finally looked up, noticing everyone she looked at Mack. Seeing the beads of sweat coming down his face and the pulsating vein on the side of his head, she knew he was angry, along with Renzo who stared at me. She looked at me and as if on cue...

"I'm pregnant!" she held the test up as she looked from me and then back at Mack, who looked like he wanted to drag the baby out of her. Out of all this shit, I just wanted to know how the fuck this nigga found my house and why the hell I didn't lock my damn door!

PANIC

Kia

We all stood there in my living room staring at Amber, whose face was turning beet red, while Mack was looking like he was about to lose his mind. He looked at Amber as if he was about to kill her. He leaned his head slightly to the side and then dropped his hands as if he was about to fight. It was like Renzo instantly caught on and quickly moved in front of Mack. Mack's eyebrows furrowed and the anger lines formed across his forehead as he tried to piece together some shit in his head. Before we could react properly, Mack pushed Renzo so hard out of the way and charged at Amber who tried to take off down the hall but was not fast enough. He reached out for her and yanked her back by her shirt. The way he slammed her against the wall, I knew he put a dent in my wall. I was surely going to curse Mack's ass out about it later. I scrambled trying to get to my cousin so I could help her, as

Yams followed behind me. I would hate for my cousin to get beat up behind my shit.

"Mack, baby please stop," Amber sobbed as the tears ran down her face.

"Bitch you had a nigga in my house? Then you let the nigga kiss you! And now I'm supposed to believe the fucking baby in your stomach is mine? Bitch I will kill you before I let you to think you going to go nine months and push out a fucking baby that don't belong to me!" he growled and at that point, I got scared and began to forcefully pull this nigga away from Amber. He had his hand around her throat. At this point as her eyes became glassy and red while he took away her oxygen.

"Mack! Please stop! It's your baby! I promise!" I yelled in Mack's ear as I struggled to pull him away. Renzo was about to help when he looked at Yams. They began to stare each other down. I quickly got up and ran for my gun because I knew Mack wasn't letting up and Amber didn't have much time before he choked her to death. I yanked the nightstand drawer open and found my loaded gun. I ran back in the hallway.

"Mack let her the fuck go before your brains be all over this damn wall!" I barked and the sound of the gun being cocked back made Mack look towards me and then back at Amber. I walked forward and pressed the cold steel gun to Mack's head.

"If she dies, you die too nigga!" I said through clenched teeth as my chest heaved up and down from being out of breath. One thing for sure, no one was getting away with hurting my cousin. We had the same blood running through our veins and no matter what, we took care of each other.

"Yo chill Kia. Mack let her go, dawg. This shit ain't worth it! She's not worth it," Renzo finally decided to say something, but that only pissed me off more.

"Nigga fuck y'all! Talking about she ain't worth it. Both of y'all niggas fucking triflin'! Now get the fuck out my shit!" I yelled. Mack finally let Amber go as she gasped for air. She had her hand around her throat struggling to get her breathing under control. Mack stood up slowly as he stared at me with a mug, but I didn't care. He crossed the line putting his hands on Amber.

As he stood there, Amber's leg went straight for Mack's balls. He yelled out in excruciating pain and I saw her punch him repeatedly on the top of his head while he held his groin. I don't know what strength Amber mustered up to began kicking ass, but I was definitely here for it because that red ring that was forming around her neck was going to be visible and hard to miss for a few days or more.

"You put your hands on me nigga and I'm carrying your seed!" Amber yelled between each hit. Mack finally was able to stand, and he shoved Amber so hard, she fell back. I pointed my gun at the nigga square between the eyes ready to put a hole in him.

"That ain't my fucking baby, and until you do one of them paternity test before the baby gets here, don't you bring your ass near my fucking house! Oh, and Kia fuck you too! Because y'all hoes are shady as fuck and to do that to Tina was fucked up! I can't believe I loved a fraud ass bitch like you! You know what the fucked up part about this shit is? I would have choose you over Tina every time, but you didn't let a nigga make that decision. You forced it and ain't shit real about what we have. Matter of fact, don't come back. I'm done with y'all grimey ass hoes!" Mack delivered a low blow of hurt to my cousin that sent her into a flood of tears. She let out a heart-breaking scream and balled up on the floor. Taking a deep breath, I slowly let my gun down as Mack stormed out of my door, while Renzo looked at me and Yams.

"Damn y'all hoes are scandalous. You talk about me? Hmph, I seen the tape and you just as guilty as your fucking cousin. Then on top of that, you fucking the enemy. Man fuck y'all whack ass bitches!" Renzo yelled and I frowned my face up ready to argue.

"Nigga, shut yo bitch ass up. You mad because your girl bossed up on yo cry baby ass," Yams stated without a thought. He mugged Renzo and that only hyped Renzo's silly ass up more! Jumping between the two, because I noticed Yams was not about to talk, especially the way he lifted his pants up and started to get in Renzo's face.

"Y'all stop! How the fuck do you even know him, Yams?" I finally questioned, realizing what Renzo said.

"This is a conversation between me and you, Kia!" Yams demanded. His eyes were cold and the look gave me chills.

I didn't want to challenge Yams, but being in Renzo's presence, I didn't want him to feel like I was choosing. So, to make myself look good, I snapped on the both of them and kicked them out of my house. I needed to get my thoughts together and deal with Amber. I felt bad for having my cousin lie for me, but I just couldn't deal with Renzo. Renzo knowing I was pregnant was going to cause more problems. I had already discussed it with Yams, because I felt like he needed to know since he was the one pursuing me on a different level, but now I was having second thoughts about him because he needed to explain himself. I never knew that they knew each other and that was a huge problem for me.

Finally, getting everyone out of my house and locking the door, I walked back down the hall to a distraught Amber. I sat on the floor and began to wrap my arms around her shoulders holding her. I felt so bad for her because she really did love Mack, but her being with Troy was something new and I couldn't believe she was crazy enough to do that wild stuff. I held Amber in my arms as she sobbed. I rubbed her hair gently as she continued to cry.

"It's all my fault," she wailed as she let the warm tears fall in my lap.

"Listen, Amber I love you, but you are going to be ok. I promise," I told her. Amber snatched her body up and stared in my face.

"Ok? Kia ok? This shit is not going to be ok. Mack left me just like he did Tina when we forced his hand, and now you have me pretending to be pregnant to save your ass. This may be a joke to you, but this shit is my real life! Mack and I were getting married!" she shouted.

"Bitch are you serious? I did that shit with Tina for you. I didn't do that shit because I wanted to. Mack is mad about the lying and deceitful shit your ass did! Not because you're pretending to be pregnant. Like get the fuck out of here with that bullshit!" I got up off the floor and mugged the hell out of my cousin because I was so sick of her accusing everyone about the shit she created. She wanted to set Tina up after I told her ass it wasn't a good idea, but me being a down ass cousin and friend, I went along with the shit and this the thanks I got. All I know was the bitch better keep her mouth shut about my damn secret until I figured out what to do.

"Well, that shit sent him over the edge!" She got up, wiping her tears as she followed behind me. "So how long you plan to keep your shit a secret because as you can see our secrets don't stay a secret for long around here!" The sarcasm dripped from her voice. It was so funny how she stopped crying instantly to get in my business. I rolled my eyes and opened the fridge, grabbing a bottle of water. I was stressed out at this moment, because I knew Amber would need to stay with me because her simple-minded ass couldn't go home to Mack's crazy self. I didn't want Amber around me, but she was indeed family and she was definitely in need of a place to stay. I decided to open the duffle bag and seeing the stacks of money along with a note stating that I was bought out, pissed me the hell off. I knew Renzo had something to do with Nadia doing this shit. I took off towards the door.

"Kia what's wrong?" Amber asked as she followed behind me.

Seeing Renzo and Yams still exchanging words, I walked towards Renzo and he looked at me. I knew he was angry because of the pulsating vein on the side of his head.

"Renzo what's up with the bag you sent me? What the fuck is that note talking about? Did you do that shit behind my back?" I questioned. I was more so hurt that he was trying to cut ties with me, even with business. I knew who ever he was with was causing this shit. I couldn't believe Vinny would have me cut off. I mean the lump sum of money was nice, but it's nothing compared to what I would have made weekly.

"Yea, we done. Especially if you're rocking with this nigga. It's either he leaves or I'm gone," he stated as a matter of fact. My right leg shook as I bit my bottom lip.

"Renzo, you don't get to make demands, and this nigga can stay if I want him to!" I advised him as I turned on my heels and began to walk away, but he grabbed my arm and firmly pulled me back. I noticed Yams came close to me. but I gave him a nod to let him know I was cool.

"That's how we rocking? Because you fuck with him, you're an enemy too," he said through clenched teeth in my ear. I leaned back and smirked. Renzo knew he fucked up because he wasn't in control anymore.

"Oh, I'm good. You made a deal to X me out of everything," I snatched away and walked towards my door with Yams following behind me.

"Kia, mark my words. You gon' regret this shit," Renzo said, but it was the way he said it, that just made my body tremble in fear. I was afraid of what Renzo was thinking or had planned. I was never afraid of Renzo, but I was more afraid of how much he loved me. Once I was inside the house, I closed the door behind Yams once he walked inside. I noticed Amber was no longer in the kitchen, which I was thankful for.

"You need to leave as soon as Renzo is gone. Nigga you been lying about shit! What are you using me to get close to Renzo or some shit? I'm good on you," I stood with my hand on my hip and my eyebrows furrowed as I looked him up and down in disgust.

"Look Kia, I'm only going to tell you this once. I never knew you fucked with that lame ass nigga until now," he began to say, and I cut him off immediately.

"What we not going to do is the name calling shit. That shit is lame as fuck," I checked him instantly, because I hated for niggas to talk shit on a nigga that wasn't around to defend themselves.

"Fuck what you talkin bout. On God, a nigga didn't know y'all was together or was affiliated with each other. Had I known, I wouldn't have caught feelings. A nigga really fucks with you, but I'm not gon lie, me and yo old nigga beefin heavy because he moved his way in to my area opening new traps," Yams broke down his and Renzo's problems. Looking at Yams confused, I didn't know anything about another trap.

"The fuck is you talking about another trap," I stated with confusion. My eyes met his and I noticed he was serious about what he was saying. I couldn't believe what I was hearing. This nigga had other traps. No wonder he didn't mind just giving me a lump sum of money to back off. He clearly was not hurting for anything.

"Apparently, you didn't know, but that just let me know the nigga can't be trusted." Yams advised shaking his head at the situation.

"Listen today has been a bit much and I need time to think. Can I call you later?" I told him, and he nodded his head in agreement. He walked over to me and took his hand to lift my chin lightly. He pecked my lips and rubbed the side of my face.

"Look for what it's worth, a nigga still fucking with you," he dropped his hand from my face and headed out the door.

I was stressed and overwhelmed because I wanted to know if what Yams said was true. I sighed deeply and walked over to my front door making sure to lock it. I walked in the back towards my bedroom and found Amber on the bed pouring her tears onto my bed soaking it as if she waisted water on it. I got close to her and we hugged each other and cried together because we both had hard decisions to deal with. While Amber tried to figure out if Mack would ever be her husband, I had a growing baby inside of me that I needed to decide, whether I was keeping or not. This day had taken a toll on the both of us, so there was only way to compensate for this, which is to cry ourselves to sleep.

CONFUSED

Mack

I sat in the car as Renzo drove in and out of traffic. I was overly stressed regarding the issue. I couldn't believe what was on that damn laptop and let's not forget the USB. This girl had cameras installed in our house to spy on me but ended up having the same cameras she had install to catch me doing something record her indiscretions. When I finally got inside the laptop, I was able to see Amber and some nigga sit in my living room, cuddled up watching movies and talking for days. I noticed she was crying on his shoulder one night and I couldn't understand how she let another nigga be her shoulder to cry on when she had fucking cousins and me. This nigga ate that shit up too. I could tell he was more of friend to Amber, but the attraction was there. The minute he kissed her; I felt my anger rise like it did when you cut the AC off in your house in Miami's summer heat. She pulled away immediately and kicked the nigga out.

I was angry, but the real hurt came when I saw what was on the USB drive. To see what Tina had been saying all along was nothing but the truth, I felt the guilt come in for how I mistreated her. Amber's fowl ass set her up and had her cousin to fucking help. They had to drug them both because the video starts with them dragging Tina and her study buddy into the bed together to make it seem like they were fucking. These hoes literally stripped them naked and placed the clothes strategically around the room. I watched Amber adjust the camera. You could hear Kia tell her why the hell she was recording it when I would just burst in and catch them in action. I was so lost and confused, I had to watch the tape over and over. I was trying to get an understanding of what I just saw. I wasn't sure how to feel, but I knew I loved Amber in the worst way because my heart ached for her. Then to know I let my anger get the best of me and it was a possibility I could have hurt my unborn child. I sat there thinking of my situation more and more while Renzo rambled on and on about Kia and Yams.

Renzo made it his business to find out where Kia lived using fucking Chase to find out. He had that nigga playing private eye detective and shit.

"Nigga, are you listening?" he finally stopped to address me.

"Naw. I'm not. Just take a nigga home I got to think," I honestly told him.

"Look, a nigga gon drop you off, but tomorrow, we got to put shit together so we can run down on these niggas," Renzo delegated. I continued my silence because I wasn't sure if I spoke it would be anything good coming out of my mouth. Sometimes Renzo didn't understand when a nigga wasn't in the damn mood. I told his ass before to check the hood out before putting those traps there, but he didn't listen. Honestly, ever since Nadia came into his life, he has been hardheaded as fuck and it was getting on my damn nerves. Finally pulling up to my house, I don't think I waited for him to put the car in park before I opened the door and jumped out.

"Damn, nigga. Don't kill yourself trying to get into the damn house. Just chill out nigga. Drink you some brown my nigga and get a bad bitch to suck yo dick. You will be ok!" Renzo said before driving off. This nigga gave horrible advice when it came to relationships. I walked inside and went straight for the bottle of Don Julio. I opened the bottle and drank straight from it, feeling the burning sensation of the liquor going down. I sat the bottle down on the counter, with thoughts of how I was going to deal with Amber. I walked into the bathroom and turned on the faucet and began filling my hands with water and throwing it on my face. I dried my face with a towel and walked back out into the kitchen. Grabbing the bottle of Don Julio, I began to down the bottle. I leaned over the kitchen counter and looked at my phone seeing that Amber was calling I decided to turn my phone off. This bitch had to be nuts if she thought I was going to talk to her. My burner phone began to ring, pulling it out I noticed it was Tina.

"Yo," I answered my phone.

"Hey, can you please come and watch your daughter while I work?" she begged. Feeling like this was the distraction I needed, I decided I would go ahead and do Tina this solid. Plus, this gave me a chance to apologize to her.

"Aight," I told her, as I got up and grabbed my other phone and keys.

"No, for real your serious?" she asked in disbelief.

"A nigga on the way," I advised her and disconnected the call.

I left the house and drove down to her house that I got her. If Amber ever found out I gave this girl the down payment for her house and still helped with the mortgage, I know she would put me six feet under. It's funny how I instantly thought about Amber, but her fucking another man was something I couldn't even handle. I finally made it to Tina's. Using the key to open the door, I heard beads going crazy in the living room. Then a scream of laughter.

"Mommy! Daddy's here!" she yelled laughing and running in my direction. I just closed the door and locked it before she made it to wrap her body around my leg squeezing it tight.

"Liyah baby. I missed you!" I picked her up planting kisses over all over her fat cheeks.

"Daddy!" she giggled and then wiggled her body to get out of my grasp. I let her down and she took off running in the opposite direction. I saw Tina dressed for work. She gave me a grateful smile.

"Thank you so much. My momma decided she rather go to the casino," she rolled her eyes at her own comment.

"She still at it hunh?" I chuckled, and she shook her head in annoyance.

"She had a bath. There are snacks in the fridge and cabinets and there is dinner on the stove. Y'all don't stay up too late." She said putting her Louis Vuitton bag on her arm.

"Hey, I need to talk to you," I told her. She looked at me confused as she raised her eyebrow.

"Um, I don't have a late shift tonight so we can talk about it when I get off," she more so asked.

Nodding my head in agreement, she smiled at me and left out the door. Hearing her lock the door with her key, I went inside the living room and decided to play with my daughter until she passed out.

These were the times I felt stress free. My daughter took away all of my worries. The smile on her fat cheeks brought a smile to my face even in my darkest days. Sometimes I wished I could have been around when she was first born, but I couldn't go back in time. I had to make the best of the time that was set before me. I played with Maliyah for hours until we both finally passed out in her bedroom. She had one foot in my mouth and her other leg was wrapped around my arm while she held on to it like it was a teddy bear. I felt a presence around me making me jump in my sleep. I looked towards the door and saw Tina sitting there taking a picture of us. Gently pulling my arm away from my daughter's body slowly, she rolled over and grabbed the pillow and snuggled in it as if it was me. I put the blanket on her and then stood up to stretch my body. I walked towards the door as Tina smiled at me.

"What are you staring at?" I asked her as I walked pass her out into the hallway.

"What? Y'all too cute. I can't help it," she giggled following behind me to the kitchen, grabbing the Hennessy off the counter and pouring me a cup.

"Oh, you drinking hard liquor at this time of night? Nigga its three in the morning," Tina said, but I didn't care about what she was talking about. My mind wouldn't get off Amber. I downed the whole cup of Hennessy and as soon as the brown liquid went down, I grunted loudly from the slight burn. I poured another cup and took that one to the head.

"Mack, what are you trying to forget? You don't drink like that unless something is really bothering you. Are you ok?" she sincerely asked.

"Look, I owe you an apology, I know the truth and I know you didn't sleep with that nigga," I told Tina. The perplexed look on her face told me she was confused about what I was saying to her.

'What are you talking about? Have you had too much to drink?" she quizzed as she looked at me suspiciously.

"I saw a video and..." I paused. I realized I couldn't tell her how I knew because if I knew Tina as well as I do, I knew she was going to be ready to fight.

"What video? Mack are you drunk?" she asked me again. I poured another cup and took It straight to the head.

"Listen, just know I found out the truth and I know you didn't cheat on me with that lil lame ass nigga," I told her, and she looked at me in disbelief.

"Really? I have been trying to tell you this forever. You said something about a video, was that what proved I was innocent?" she questioned me. I became more annoyed because I was not up to discussing the logistics. She just needed to know I apologized and that was it.

"Drop it, Tina," I told her before grabbing the rest of the Henny bottle and heading back to the room with my daughter. Mid way to me making it to my daughter's room door, I felt Tina's hand tug me. I looked back at her and eyed her from head to toe.

"What's wrong with you?" she sincerely asked.

"I'm good. I just need to lay down." I told her opening the door to Maliyah's room. I could tell she wanted to say something, but I really didn't want her to get any ideas that we were going to discuss or do anything. "Goodnight," I told her before going into the room.

"Mack, all I'm going to say is don't let my child wake up to your Henny breath, let alone the whole bottle in the room," she scoffed and walked off mumbling something under breath. Just that quick Tina's so called compassion went out the window. I heard her slam her room door and decided since I did have the bottle, I would go downstairs and drown my problems away. A nigga was heartbroken.

The sound of moans made me open my heavy eyes. I felt wetness wrapped around my dick and moans from a woman. Looking down the smiles from Amber as she topped me off made me smirk. She was sucking my dick like she had a point to prove the feeling had my toes curling as she brought me to a climax. She crawled up to me as my vision became slightly blurry. It felt warm and wet as she slid down on me and began to rock in a steady motion. Her moans turned me on more.

"Mack, Mack, Mack!" I heard another voice calling me. The sting from being slapped made me really open my eyes. I looked in the face of Tina who looked slightly irritated.

"Nigga you over here dreaming about this girl while you on my couch with a damn hard on! You better be glad your daughter sleeps late! She still in bed knocked out. Nigga you want breakfast?" She leaned on her right leg with her hand on her hip. She had on some little shorts and a tank that made her nipples prominent through the shirt. They were standing at attention. Her ass cheeks dropped from under the shorts like they were playing peekaboo. Tina was a mocha complexion with a curly short cut. She was a very pretty girl with hazel eyes. I stared at her and rubbed my dick in a downward position. I was trying to contain him, but the way Tina was looking, I wasn't sure I could hold out much longer. Especially with a nigga feeling down and shit. I got up off the couch and fell back down on the couch. I realized I was feeling a little light head from the alcohol I had last night.

"You ok?" She asked.

"A niggas good. I just feel a little dizzy," I truthfully told her. She walked over to me. She placed her hand on my forehead and then grabbed my face looking in my eyes.

"Your eyes look a little dilated. Did you take any pills when you were drinking?" She asked me as she walked away to the kitchen.

"Naw, I just smoked with Renzo before I came here yesterday," I leaned my head back on the couch and closed my eyes. I felt Tina's presence over me. I opened my eyes and noticed she was looking at her watch and placed the round part of the stethoscope on my chest as she listened to my heartbeat and monitored her watch. With Tina finally passing her exam and officially being a nurse with a bachelors, she felt that she could cure anyone. I was low key proud of her because now she was back in school to get her masters, she was aiming to be a Nurse Practitioner, but the outside looking in would think she was dumb and ghetto because of how she acted a lot of the times. Not sure how she acted at work, but outside of work sometimes I wanted to go upside her damn head.

"Well your heart rate is ok. I think you should relax for now," she said as she was just about to move. I grabbed her hand, pulling her back so she could fall in my lap. My hard on poked her and I could hear her clear her throat as she tried to gather her thoughts. "Mack, you don't look well. I think you should just chill a little bit," her voice was small and timid.

"Honestly, I just still feel like it's from all the drinking I did last night, but right now I need you." I pretty much begged. I needed the hurt to go away from Amber. The sexual tension began to rise, but I saw the sadness in Tina's eyes. I knew if we crossed those boundaries, it was going to be hard to go back. Honestly, Tina was my first real love and first real girlfriend. She taught me things that I was able to carry over into my current relationship with Amber. The saying that sometimes women make the man better for another woman is so true, because Tina made me a better man for Amber. My phone rang bringing me back to reality. Seeing it was Amber, I hit the ignore button. At that point I decided to head home. I was this close to probably making the biggest mistake. Tina got up annoyed and turned around to head back into the kitchen. I could have sworn she wiped her eyes as if she was crying, but I didn't want to ask, and I really didn't want to know if she was really crying.

"Look I'm going to head home. Hit me if Maliyah needs anything," I told her and got up to leave. I headed towards the door hoping that today would be a better day, because I felt like something bad was going to happen. Especially after looking at the fifty missed calls from Amber since last night. I waited a few seconds to see if Tina would say anything, but she didn't. She began to busy herself in the kitchen and ignoring my existence. Shaking my head, I walked out the door without another word.

BAIT!

Renzo

Waking up in an empty house was not something I could get used to. Nadia was still out of town. Kia was fucking on my enemy and a nigga didn't have any side bitches to get his dick wet with. I leaned forward and stretched thinking about the day I dropped Mack off. It had been about a week since then. My nigga was so fucked up that he had been dodging me. I had to set my plan in motion to get at Yams by myself. I knew Kia was messing around with him, but she would have to be a casualty of war. I got up and brushed my teeth, flossed and gargled with Listerine. I was very particular about my mouth. I showered and dressed in some g-star jeans, a plain white v-neck and my Louis Vuitton slides. I never was a crazy fan of designer until I met Nadia. I preferred the chilled looks with occasional designers, like I had to have the latest sneakers, and my jewelry game had to be on point. I did rock the designer belts, but the clothes and the shoes were not something I used to be in until now. I grabbed my phone, gun and the roll of money sitting on my bedside and left from out of the house, being sure to lock the door.

I drove to the A.P.T's and it felt like home. I missed living over here. Soon as I stepped out of the whip, I smelled the chicken grease and the sounds of laughter coming from kids along with hair beads bouncing to the beat of feet that were running. I really missed the way this place came alive during the day and at night. I saw Sashay and she was just the person I was looking for. I noticed she sat on the staircase with a book in her hand, reading. She looked up and our eyes met. She gave an inviting smile and I walked over. I stood over as she looked up at me with her deep inviting piercing eyes.

"What brings you over here? I thought I didn't have to do a run for a while," she questioned, while looking at me. The glare from the sun peeping through the trees must have aggravated her because before I answered she put her head down again.

"I was looking for you," I smoothly responded as I eyed her seductively.

"Oh no nigga, I'm not dealing with that crazy dog of yours," she referred to Kia. I scrunched my face up instantly turned off and becoming agitated with her choice of words.

"A nigga don't fuck with Kia, but I didn't want that little pussy anyway. A nigga just need you for a job. I'm willing to pay a hefty amount if the job is done right." I truthfully told her.

"What happen with you and Kia?" she was now more intrigued into what I was talking about.

"To keep it a hundred, it ain't for you to know. I just need to know if you want to make this paper," I asked her. Her eyebrows furrowed as I could tell she was immediately offended, but I could care less. I didn't want to talk about Kia.

"Nigga, you don't have to be so rude. I was trying to be a concerned friend," she pouted as she looked back into her book.

"Girl, you ain't no concern friend. You trying to see what's up so you can be a fuck friend."

Looking at the shock look on her face, I knew I was right. My bluntness was necessary because nine times out of ten, people couldn't handle it.

"Nigga, fuck you! Next time I won't ask shit about you. I will do what you need me to do if the price is right," she went back to the subject at hand.

"Good, so it's paying two bands. Is that cool with you?" I asked her and she nodded her head in agreement. What I did like about Sashay it didn't matter what you asked her to do, she didn't ask what it was she needed to do, she always agreed long as I made sure she was straight financially. My phone rang interrupting me and Sashay's conversation. Seeing it was my brother Ricardo I answered.

"Yoooo!" I answered.

"Nigga, where you at? We got a serious problem." Ricardo sounded mad and aggravated.

"Bro, everything good?" I was feeling anxious because my gut was telling me some shit happened.

"Nigga, just pull up on T3," he responded in code, right before disconnecting the call. We called the third trap house T3 in code. The confused look on my face as I stared at my phone, made Sashay jump up.

"Is everything ok? You need me to drive?" she offered.

"Just come roll with me. Something must have happened," I told her, and she got up cradling the book to her chest. We jumped in my whip and headed in the direction of the T3 trap. I had this bad feeling that something happened that was not good. I pulled up in front of the house and parked diagonally, being sure to be close to the sidewalk. Ricardo was yelling at one of the niggas as Sashay and I got out of the car.

"Yo nigga what's going on?" I was visibly lost, and I needed to know what was going on.

"Man, some niggas came when Chase and I was on our way back to pick up the money. The niggas took everything Renz. This shit was a setup.

They knew exactly where to go and how to get these stupid ass niggas distracted."

"Nigga what? You telling me my money gone?" I barked. My anger was on another level. One thing I didn't like is for someone to fuck with my money and I worked too hard to get to where I was now. My fist was balled up ready to knock my brother's head loose. This was why I needed Mack. I loved my brother, but Mack was my right hand. Grabbing my phone trying to calm down, I dialed Mack numbers. Hearing his voice come through the phone, I knew he wasn't ok. He didn't sound good at all.

"Mack! I need you to pull it together because nigga I need you down at T3 now. We got fucking jacked!" I yelled in the phone. Before I could say another word, Mack disconnected the call and knowing him, he was on his way. "Nigga where's Chase?" I questioned.

"He's inside checking them niggas," he answered. I could tell Ricardo was feeling some type of way because I called Mack, but the truth of the matter was my brother wasn't into running traps. His thing was guns. He was the nigga you called when it was time to do a drill. "Look just let me just put these lil niggas brains on the floor because how the hell these niggas get jacked is beyond me.

"Wait so none of these niggas was shot?" My curiosity was heightened at this point.

"I think it was to send a message," Chase walked over and said. He stood next to Ricardo with his hand in his pockets, looking annoyed. "Nigga said we need to move or next time it will be dead bodies. I told you let's just run down on them niggas. One good drill and them niggas won't talk no more," Chase was hyped up at this point. Him and Ricardo were one in the same, but I promise I thought Chase was worse.

"Hey, Renzo. Some girl is calling your phone. It said Nadia and she keeps calling. Its be ringing non-stop." Sashay came out of the car and said. Chase smirked at me and shook his head.

"Nigga, Nadia? Not Vince's niece Nadia?"
Ricardo screwed his face up so hard, I thought his
nose was going to be in the middle of his eyes. I
walked off ignoring him, because I was going to see
what he knew about her, because the way he asked,
I knew he knew something. I grabbed my cell phone
from Sashay, who didn't seem bothered. She had
her head back in the book. Before I could even call
Nadia, she was calling me back.

"Yo!" I snapped, answering the phone.

"Renzo, I don't like the fact I have to call
you a million times for you to answer," she calmly
spoke. Nadia never yelled or raised her voice no
matter how mad she got, far as I knew. I never seen
it.

"Yo a nigga handling something. Let me hit
you back." My attitude was evident.

"What's going on?" she spoke before I
could disconnect the call.

"Look, I will tell you when you get back," I
said hanging up before she could even respond. I
must have hit a nerve because Nadia began blowing

my phone up again. Silencing it so it would not bother Sashay, I gave it back to her and walked back over to Chase and my brother.

"So, what you want to do?" Chase asked ready for whatever.

"Look, they got to us before we got to them, so they are really going to expect us to come at them, but we are going to use Sashay as bait," I revealed my plan to Chase and Ricardo. Mack's car pulled up and he was madder than me because they were really tapping into his money because he got more profit from this trap.

"Yo, I know them niggas in there bet not be alive?" Mack mugged Ricardo and Chase.

"Just chill Mack. We going to get rid of these niggas because something about this shit don't sit right anyway," I honestly spoke. I could tell by the looks we all agreed them niggas needed to be gone. We were going to send them nigga's they different ways and follow them to see who was running they mouth.

"Someone knew we were not here," Chase commented.

"Renzo, I told you this shit was going to happen, but you wouldn't listen. This nigga is about to test you, so what you going to do?" Mack tried to test my gangster.

"We going to body them niggas," I simply said. I was going to go along with my plan in getting rid of Yams and his crew. No more playing nice. After sitting outside for an hour talking to Ricardo, Mack, and Chase, we decided to link up to put the plan in motion. We agreed for a date and I jumped in the car and left. My phone started ringing while I was driving. Looking down seeing it was Nadia again, I instantly became annoyed.

"Yo!" I answered.

"Renzo what's going on with you?" Nadia firmly asked.

"Honestly, I don't understand you calling me so much. You call more than I can think, but for what? My answers are never going to change," I snapped on the phone.

"Please calm your tone. I was letting you know I will be home tomorrow. See you then." She disconnected the call. I knew I had pissed her off, but I had enough of her harassing me and calling all day.

"So, you went and got another girl worse than Kia?" Sashay chuckled as her eyes stayed glued into the book.

"Well, I guess you can say that now. Kind of hard to explain," I told her. I looked over and noticed she never looked up from the book.

"What are you reading that you haven't looked up yet?" I asked her and she smiled at me.

"Well, you kind of made fun of me being a waist of a person, and ever since then, I decided I needed to do more than what I was doing, so I went back to school and I'm reading this book for my literature class." She proudly said. I looked at her and smiled because I always knew Sashay could do better if she applied herself.

"Dang, that's what's up," I told her. I didn't want to sound dry, but I just lost money and I knew it was because of that nigaga Yams. I was going to pull up on Kia because I needed to talk to her about this nigga one more time.

"Look, whatever the issue is Renzo, you know a bitch is down for you, even if you a fucked-up nigga at times." Sashay said. I knew she was kissing my ass because she wanted a nigga to pipe her down like old times. I had every intention to do so, but a nigga needed to run down on Kia first. I pulled back up to the A.P.T's and dropped Sashay off. I started driving to Kia's house. Ten minutes into driving, I noticed someone following me. I switched lanes for the third time and noticed the truck still following me. The truck looked like one of Vinny's people. I just knew this girl didn't have them following me. Instead of continuing my drive to Kia's, I exited and made my way to the condo that me and Nadia shared. Soon as I pulled up to valet, I noticed the truck park on the side. I made sure my hammer was in my back tucked in my pants. I gave the valet guy my keys and got out. I discreetly walked the opposite direction so I could run up on the truck. When I was close enough, I pulled my gun out and used it to tap on the window. The driver let the window down slow and put their hands up with a smirk. I instantly recognized it was on of Nadia's bodyguards.

"She really got y'all following me?" I snapped. The pussy ass cracker looked at me and smirked.

"Following orders," he shrugged. Pissed off wasn't even the word. I put the gun down and then tucked it in pants in my back. Shaking my head at the white man, I walked off and headed in the house. I needed to sneak out to talk to Kia, without these fuckers following me.

Making it inside the house, I pulled my phone out ready to go in on Nadia. My phone rung. Seeing Mack's name, I answered the phone.

"Nigga, this shit got to get handled ASAP." I could tell Mack been drinking. He had been a mess since the whole shit with Amber.

"Mack we will, just chill. I know you ain't drinking?" I asked him.

"What else can I do?" he sounded defeated.

"Nigga, fuck these hoes. I'm going to check on the other traps and then I'm going to slide up on you," I told him before disconnecting the call. I called Nadia again, but I got no answer. Getting frustrated I decided to call Chase and Ricardo to pull up on me, so I could get past my personal hired stalker. After about fifteen minutes, they were downstairs. Advising them to pull up a block away from the condo, I was going to sneak out one the other exits to get away from the person Nadia hired to watch me. The amount of time it took to shake the bodyguard only pissed me off more. When I got in the car Ricardo and Chase decided to crack me.

"Nigga Nadia's ass is worse than Kia," Ricardo laughed.

"That nigga thought his grass was going to be greener," Chase cackled. I gave the nigga a nasty look ready to curse both of their asses out, even if they were telling the truth.

"Naw he thought the grass was going to be a pretty green with no effort. He forgot he has to deal with all the troubles of keeping the grass a pretty green. Nigga should have left that crazy bitch where she stood," he spoke how he feel.

"Ric, what you know? You keep making sly comments," I questioned him.

"All I know is the bitch is not wrapped too tight and if she does not get what she wants, let's just say it always ends up her way," he said seriously. "I know a nigga that used to fuck with her and had to stop because she was having him followed and had become more controlling." Ricardo said.

"Well who is this nigga, because she's the type that don't look like she even like the niggas you know." I wasn't trying to put my brother down, but it was facts. Nadia was on a different level.

"Honestly, nigga he looks like you, and people use to say we looked a like. Shit the nigga favored you more to me, but after they broke-up, no one has seen him since. Shit I wasn't close with the nigga so I couldn't tell you much, but when I did see him, he looked fucking stressed all the time because she was always calling and pulling up." Ricardo seemed unfazed about the information he was delivering, but for me, I was hanging on his every word. I needed to know if this girl was crazy for real. I mean nothing scared me, so she had met her match, but I didn't want to deal with a nagging bitch all the time. She did have people in high places. It was easy for her to make a body disappear.

"Nigga, don't sweat that shit. She has to come through an army to get to you and plus, I think you giving her a run for her money," he chuckled, but I didn't find it funny. We made it to Mack's house and pulled up to the scene of him and Amber going toe to toe outside. Kia sat in Mack's face arguing with him as well. Getting out the car, I could hear Amber going off about Tina.

"Nigga, I don't give a fuck what I did. You bet not have fucked that bitch or I promise you, I'm going to kill her!" She screamed from the top of her lungs. I knew for a fact the neighbors were going to come outside.

"Amber, shut up!" Kia tried to get between the two.

"Fuck this baby I'm going to kill it! I will be dammed if I deal with you sleeping at that bitches house! I know your ass is too!" she screamed again. I saw Mack's eyes get dark as he charged at her and his hand wrapped around her throat. I saw Kia try to pry Mack away from her, but she was too small. She began punching him in the side of the head but with the type of anger Mack had, her punches were not making him move. Chase, Ricardo and I ran towards them trying to stop the altercation before nine was called. Ricardo and Chase pulled Mack as Kia and I pulled Amber back. When Mack finally let her go, she began coughing uncontrollably trying to regain her breathing.

"Yo Mack, just calm down nigga!" I yelled as Ricardo and Chase pulled him into the house.

"This shit crazy," I said out loud but more to myself. Amber broke down in my arms and for the first time I felt bad for her. Looking up at Kia who was trying to catch her breath, but the hickey on her neck made me want to slap the bitch. I frowned my face and she looked at me and rolled her eyes. I watched her walk inside the house, and I continued to console Amber. I saw Kia come back out a few minutes later with what look like to be Amber's clothes.

"All this shit mine in this shit! That shit ain't hers!" Mack's silly ass yelled at Kia. I could tell they were still holding him down because he sounded out of breath. This nigga was tripping. The girl was pregnant and didn't need the added stress.

"Yo Mack, shut the fuck up!" I shouted. Amber began crying harder in my chest. This shit was a mess. I wish Amber's crazy ass never did this silly shit. I saw Kia march back inside without a care in the world, unphased of Mack's threats.

"What am I supposed to do?" Amber whined and I honestly didn't know. I couldn't understand what made Amber think what she did was ok. Especially setting up Tina. These girls get wilder and wilder if you ask me.

"Look, pull yourself together. I mean did you fuck the nigga?" I questioned her and she shook her head no. "No offense is the baby really his?" I asked her and her head went up and down confirming it was Mack's baby. "Look let me go inside. I will be right back," I advised her. I headed in the house brushing past Kia, who looked like she was glowing.

"Y'all niggas get off me. I'm calm!" Mack shouted.

"Nigga take that base out your mouth and maybe we will believe you," Chase smirked. They continued to hold Mack's ass down, as Kia went back and forth until she felt like she got everything she needed for her cousin.

"Mack, you childish as fuck. It's sad that people can't be civilized. If you put your hands on my cousin one more time, I promise on everything I love, we will be visiting you in the hospital and that's on my dead grandma!" Kia stated

"Fuck you Kia!" he yelled back, but she already slammed the front door soon as she walked out. As soon as we heard Kia's truck doors close, Chase and Ricardo let him go. He hopped up mad ready to fight Ricardo and Chase.

"Mack, chill. Save that energy for them niggas," I told him, and he mugged them both, but they could careless.

"Mack let me ask you something. Why you keep putting your hands on your pregnant fiancé?" I couldn't understand the logic of why he kept putting his hands on a pregnant woman.

"Man, I have been trying so hard to not kill her ass, but every time I look at her, she makes me want to lay her ass out in a box and dig her a grave."

"Yo nigga. You silly as fuck. You can't get mad that the bitch has one up on you" Chase chuckled.

"Nigga I never cheated on her," Mack frowned his face.

"Ok nigga, you haven't cheated since you proposed?" Chase came with the comeback that silenced Mack.

"Fuck you!" Mack spat and we all cracked up laughing, but him. He wore a scowl on his face.

"Nigga, so let me get this straight. You let your bitch walk out the door, with Kia's single as fuck ass, to go to a house that don't have surveillance so you can watch her and she pregnant but you not sure it's yours? Yea nigga you dumb as fuck. I wouldn't give two fucks. I would have this bitch in here locked up until the DNA is done." Chase chuckled. He was clearly amused by the situation.

"Dat nigga about to watch that new nigga feed his baby," Ricardo laughed.

"Man, that nigga going to be right there to help them feed the baby. You know Mack's lowkey psycho," Chase laughed.

"Y'all niggas lame as fuck. Ain't shit about to happen," Mack frowned as he rapidly typed in his phone. He was texting so fast, he never looked up. We all stood there watching him.

"What she say nigga?" Chase smirked, and we all laughed because we knew who he was texting even if he didn't want to bring it up. My phone rang and I noticed it was Nadia. I instantly became annoyed.

"Yo," I answered.

"Baby, listen I'm sorry about earlier," she softly spoke.

"Save that shit. You got people following me and shit?" I questioned.

"Look, I needed to know if you were still messing with Kia," she sighed deeply.

"You told me to dead the situation, but you deaded it for me, so what else can a nigga do now but live and trap," I honestly spoke. I noticed Mack got up and disappeared to the kitchen.

"Listen, I know you have history, but it's time to make new memories that we can share. Stop living in the past it's time to move forward," she more so told me. What I have learned about Nadia, nothing was ever asked, everything was a demand. It's like I loved and hated that shit.

"Look, I will see you when you come home, and just make sure you make it worth my while," I finessed.

"Hmmmm I got you Renzy," she sweetly sad before disconnecting the call. That's what made me like Nadia. If she kept that up, we would be good.

"So, listen we run down on them niggas Friday night. Chase, keep an eye out on them to see if anything changes, and do you still got your homie working on the inside?" I pulled the pre rolled joint I had earlier.

"Yea nigga, so we good. Just make sure Mack's head is in the game," he advised, and as if on cue Mack walked back in with a bottle of Hennessey.

"Aye nigga let this be your last drink until you figure your shit out," I got up and told him. I nodded my head towards Chase and Ricardo, letting them know it was time to leave.

"Man don't worry about me. Worry about your shit, especially with the nigga you want dead sniffing up Kia's ass." He countered while downing the cup full of liquor. Letting this slick comment slide, I mugged the hell out of Mack and walked out his house with Ricardo and Chase.

"This nigga has lost his mind," Chase said to no one in particular.

"Indeed, he has," I responded as we all headed to the whip and got in. Ricardo turned the music up and we drove off to the speakers blaring Jeezy. I knew Mack was depressed about Amber; I just hoped by Friday he could have his emotions in check.

THE LOVE I HAVE FOR YOU

Amber

I was laid out on the couch, in my thick
hospital socks, cotton sweats and a plain white t-
shirt. I had my hair balled up in a bun. I needed my
weave taken down, but the way I was feeling I
didn't want to do a thing. My lips were chapped, my
eyes were puffy, and I lost plenty of weight because
my appetite had not come back. My mother
continued to call me, but I was not in the mood. I
was watching the *Twilight* movies over and over
again, feeling every emotion Bella went through.
The house was dark, and I had the covers pulled up
over me. I had an ice cream sandwich in my hand
taking small bites. I heard Kia on the phone
giggling like a schoolgirl. It had been a few days
since I last seen Mack. It was Friday and I was
home going through Mack withdrawals.

"OMG, Amber you cannot sit in this house
like this!" Kia ranted while opening the blinds
letting the sun in. She sniffed the air then covered

her nose. "Bitch, I know your ass ain't stinking up my brand new couch? Get your funky ass up and take a shower," She fumed stomping back down the hall. I heard her room door slam, and I rolled my eyes as I laid my head back down taking more bites of my ice cream sandwich. While she was in the honeymoon stages with a new man, she was moody as fuck as well with a baby in her stomach. My phone had been ringing constantly because the roles had reversed. Whatever happened when I went to get my clothes, Mack had been blowing me up ever since. According to Kia, the roles had reversed, and I had the upper hand, so I better drag that nigga while I could. I was happy Mack had not shown up here because if he did, I don't know if I could just ignore him. I missed him something terrible. I heard Kia's bedroom door open again. She stood in front of me with her hand on her hip. I continued eating my ice cream sandwich.

"Girl I know you see me here. Look we're going out and I don't want to hear shit. Get your stanking ass in the shower!" She snapped.

"You can't go with Heaven?" I whined, because I wanted to just lay here watching T.V.

"Girl, let me tell you something. You either going to go home and fix your shit or boss up on that nigga! Yea you were dead wrong, but how long you going to beat yourself up about it? One thing for sure and two things for certain, a nigga gon' do him the minute you not around. I bet you that nigga is blowing your phone up while he was with that bitch! Fuck these niggas! You haven't been to work and shit. Don't let this nigga be your downfall while he come up off what you taught him!" Kia gave it to me raw. It was funny how she had become the big cousin just that quick.

"You schooling me, but what about that baby in your stomach?" I sassed. She frowned her face at the mention of the baby.

"Girl I'm not having no baby from Renzo's trick ass. I made my appointment. I'm just waiting to go cock my legs up on these people table! Nigga won't keep me with no damn baby. I got the first morning appointment for these people to gut me like a fish," Kia's crazy ass said. She could be so insensitive at times, but I couldn't help but to laugh. This girl was crazy.

"Damn, Kia you have to act like that," I chuckled.

"Girl, I'm damaged goods right now. Renzo got some bitch that got him moving funny. He bought me out and now I don't know what to do with myself!" She confessed. I saw the hurt in her eyes and that would explain why she was running around with Yams even more lately.

"Kia maybe you should tell Renzo. I mean he deserves to know", I offered my honest opinion in my sincerest voice.

"And tell him I don't want it and it's going to be dead before he can breathe? Girl bye I'm not entertaining this. Just get yourself together, and you better be ready before me," she said without a care in the world, but I knew my cousin. She was hurt that she had to do this, and the jokes were a constant sign of trying to detach herself from the unborn child. It was a defense mechanism. She was making her way down the hall towards her bedroom when my phone rang again, but the contact name made me smile.

"Hello," I sweetly answered.

"Damn, so we kiss, and you don't answer a nigga call till now?" He chuckled.

"Nigga, I'm sure you heard the drama. Yams can't keep shit to himself," I advised him whiling rolling my eyes as if he was here. In the short time of hanging out with Yams, I learned that him and Troy were really close. They were practically brothers from another mother. Blood couldn't make them closer. Yams was always running his mouth to Troy about everything. They were each other's left and right.

"You know I'm going to know! Just in case a nigga got to hang out a window because of y'all ex niggas." He slightly laughed. I knew they were beefing with Mack and Renzo, but I appreciated how they both kept that street shit where it was.

"Nigga stop. Ain't shit poppin for you to do all that," I more so tried to convince myself than him because I knew Mack was going to show up real soon if I kept declining his calls.

"Aight, Don't say I didn't warn yo ass, but I'm on my way yo! I will be there in about twenty minutes," he stated before disconnecting the call. I was stunned because he abruptly hung up. After realizing he said he was on his way, I jumped up and took off down the hall to shower and to fix my appearance. The way my socks made me glide on Kia's clean wooden floors, my ass fell before I could make it to the guest bedroom. I real life got up looking around like someone could see me.

"Oh, bitch I heard your small ass fall on that hard floor. Hope your skinny ass didn't break a hip for that nigga" she cackled from in her room. I sucked my teeth and slowly got up off the floor, limping my ass inside the spare bedroom to get my life together before this man showed up.

I rubbed some oil on the edge part of my wig and slowly removed it. Taking my nude cap off and removing my braids, I looked in the mirror and for once I could see how I looked so drained and tired. My eyes looked like I hadn't slept in days. Turning on the shower, I stepped inside. The hot water hit my skin, make me deeply sigh in relief. I needed this hot shower to help destress me. I washed my thick curly hair that was a little past my shoulders in its natural state and then washed my body making sure not leave not one spot untouched. When I finished, I brushed my teeth and put some leave-in conditioner in my hair. I decided to put on a cute backless Maxi dress, with my Louis Vuitton tote and sandals. I left my hair curly but made sure to use the diffuser when I blow dried my hair. I did a light beat to my face, even though I didn't need it. I was on a role of making myself pretty and I was starting to feel better.

"Girl, you not ready yet? We been waiting on your ass an extra thirty minutes. The hell you doing in here?" Kia came inside the bathroom ranting.

"Just chill," I turned around to face her and she stood back, sizing me up.

"Well, damn bitch maybe I need to change."
Kia rubbed her hair back, looking like she felt self-
conscious.

"I mean, if you want to look like the nigga,"
I honestly told her. I looked Kia over and she had
on some jogger pants that looked to be Renzo's, a
fitted crop top, and her hair was pulled up in a
messy bun.

"I look that bad?" she looked down at her
clothes.

"Girl, go put on a maxi dress on and stop
acting like you about to go hug the block," I pushed
her towards the door. She reluctantly went to
change her clothes. I continued to primp in the
mirror and in ten minutes, she was walking back in
the room looking better. The white long cotton
fitted dress laid on her curves like it was meant to
be there. The dresses flowed down to my cousin's
feet, barely touching the ground. Her hair was the
same as earlier, lifted in a high messy bun. She
looked like she had swooped some baby hairs on
her edges. I grabbed her hand and made her sit on

the toilet I did a light beat of makeup to her face and it only enhanced my cousin's beauty.

"I have to admit, when you look girlie, baby you a jaw dropper," I told her she stood up looking in the mirror.

"Damn, I do look good," she admitted, while she turned side to side checking herself out in the mirror.

"You do, now let's go and make sure you put on some cute shoes," I demanded. She cut her eye at me and walked off. I had a feeling this girl was going to leave the house in something crazy. Walking out into the living room, I seen Troy's fine self sitting on the barstool in his phone. As bad as I needed to stay away from him, I wanted to be close to him. Don't get me wrong, I loved Mack, but I knew how Mack was and my actions may have cost me my relationship in ways I could never get it back.

"Damn you look good. I thought we were just grabbing food," he smirked. I walked closer to him and he stood up tall over me, putting his hand in the small of my back and pulling my closer to him. He then hugged me tight and pecked my cheek. My cheeks turned a rose red from how hard I was blushing.

"I missed you," he truthfully said, and I looked into his eyes as my body warmed up on the inside at the thought.

"I missed you too," I smiled.

"Well what about this?" Kia came out in the living room with some Burberry sneakers that were half white and with the distinct known Burberry print on the other half. Along with the matching Burberry print bag. She had a Burberry button up tied around her waist. With some shades. She was cute, but I hated that she had to have on sneakers.

"Better than earlier. Where is Yams?" I asked way too soon because her phone chimed, and she looked at it and her eyes said it all. I could tell Kia liked Yams a lot, but it wasn't the same as it was with her and Renzo. I felt like Yams was her breath of fresh air, but Renzo was her heart.

"He outside. Let's all ride together." She said, and Troy nodded in agreement.

We all walked out of the house with Kia being last, since she had to lock the door. We piled up in Yams AMG GLC. The seats were custom made in red and black and they felt good against my body. I got comfortable in my seat and we drove off to the sounds of MoneyBagg coming through the speakers. I knew Yams was paid, but I think his money was longer than Renzo's.

"Damn, you're going to kill my eardrums and no one wants to hear this!" Kia turned down his music and grabbed his phone disconnecting it from the Bluetooth.

"Girl and no one wants to listen to y'all women coochie empowerment songs y'all been on lately," his snobbish response made Kia stick the middle finger at him.

"Yams, haven't you learned anything yet? I love trap music!" She tilted her head at him. He shook his head as he smiled paying attention to the road.

The beat of Young Dolph song *Get Paid* blasted through the speakers of the car. Kia was hyped bouncing and dancing in her seat turned up. I laughed as she rapped to the lyrics from the top of her lungs.

Rule number 1, get the money first
Rule number 2, don't forget to get the money
Play by these rules and everything will be okay
Still in my trap, flipping my Frito-Lays
Go get the money, it ain't nothing else important to me
I showed her a Xanax, she hurried up and took
I fucked her so good, she got up and started cooking
Rolling up big blunts, out a pound of cookies
If you ain't got 40 bands, then you can't book me
Pulled up on the side of your bitch, she wouldn't stop looking
That bitch good as tooken, good as gone

I guarantee tonight my nigga, that bitch ain't

coming home

I got money to count, I got bitches to fuck

I got packs to flip, pistols to bust

When I was small, I ain't have nothing

Started selling dope, and prayed to God for

a plug

He showed up and said

Get paid, young nigga, get paid!

Kia was dancing in her seat and slightly lean forward tooting her booty up twerking. The fact that Yams hit the brakes and she flew further into the dashboard and then back to the seat. We all cried laughing as Kia folded her arms and pouted.

"Yams really? What if I would have got seriously hurt?" Kia rolled her eyes and huffed.

"You alright. I didn't even hit the brakes that hard," Yams smirked as he placed his hand on her stomach. Kia pouted even more as she sat back in her seat. I shook my head at her shenanigans. She could be so extra at times.

"Nigga, it doesn't matter I could have been injured and you would have been taking care of me," she sassed. Kia's personality with Yams and Renzo was different. With Yams she was always acting like a baby, and the dumb ass nigga was eating it up being sweet on her. While with Renzo, she was always on edge and always fighting. I don't remember the last time she loosened up this much around a man. Renzo was that once upon a time, but now Yams was doing it. I watched how Yams was being soothing as he rubbed her stomach and moved to her thigh rubbing it, then grabbing her hand and kissed the back of it. He was what she needed at the moment.

Pulling up to valet parking across the street, we all got out of the car and made our way into Uncut Miami. I watched Yams hold Kia's hand. Troy grabbed mine as we were escorted to our seats. The place was decorated ok, nothing to fancy, but the simplicity of it made it look good. Blue couches were wrapped around the tables to section off the areas, and they had large plasmas on the wall. After placing our orders, the hookah girl came out with our hookah, and then our two bottles came. We began to enjoy each other's company and the vibe was good. Troy sipped his drink as he stared at me.

"What?" I blushed.

"You so damn pretty sitting in front of me, and I like you with no weave." He sat back and licked his thick full lips, making my mouth water for a kiss.

"Thank you, but I don't know about giving up my weaves nigga. I already made an appointment to get a new wig install, so don't speak to soon." I honestly spoke.

"Man, I'm going to cut that shit out." He frowned his face as I burst into laughter. I looked over at Kia who had Yams sucking her face off. I could tell what ever beef he had with Renzo; my cousin didn't give two fucks about.

By the time an hour passed we were turnt up. Even though Kia was barely sipping and smoking because of her pregnancy, you would have sworn sis had a whole damn bottle the way she was cutting up to the music. She was dancing on me and Yams. We were having a really good time. Kia was winding her waist to the beat of the music as she continued to dance in front of me. She was turning around slowly to the beat of the Chris Brown song that blared through the speakers. When she looked up the look of fear made me look in her direction. I saw Mack walk in but when I saw short ass Tina right behind him, my anger rose instantly. It's like Mack knew someone was watching him. He looked over and our eyes met. He first had this look that I missed so much. The one that was always happy to see me, but when he finally noticed I was with Troy, he took off in my direction with his baby mama hot on his heels.

"You pregnant and drinking?" he grilled me. I saw the vein on the side of his head going crazy. Forgetting I had the cup of alcohol in my hand, I push it towards Kia who happily took it. Troy stood up next to me and leaned in my ear asking if I was straight. Mack's eyes grew big and before I could blink, he snatched me up by my arm. Troy was about to grab me, but Mack pulled me too fast. Kia had to jump between Troy and me.

"Troy chill. I got this," Kia said.

"Chill? This nigga is trying it," Troy calmly spoke. I could tell he was getting upset, but I didn't know what to do or say. Now things began to really go left when Kia saw Renzo and this exotic looking chick walk in looking cozy. She noticed them before they noticed what was really going on. The way Renzo dropped home girl's hand, I knew Renzo was mad he was caught up. Walking towards us they stood behind Mack.

"You got to be fucking kidding me. This what you doing now? Nigga you was that desperate!" Kia snapped. She wore a frown on her face, and I could tell she was hurt and confused. It's like everything stopped and all eyes were on us. Kia stood in disbelief, but the hurt was very evident.

"Damn, the plug Renzo? It makes sense now. The new clothes, the new attitude, the switch up. So were y'all fucking when we all first met?" Kia asked as her eyes darted back and forth between the girl and Renzo. The girl remained silent the whole time, but her presence was extremely felt.

"Kia, look we can talk later," Renzo tried to de-escalate the situation.

"So you played me nigga. You had a bitch so lost and not understanding what was wrong with us, but the whole time you building more than a work bond with this bitch," Kia chuckled and normally that mean it came with destruction.

"Bitch? You mean boss baby, and last time I checked you been let go," The exotic chick said and that only pissed me off.

"Bitch, and we will lay your white ass the fuck out too!" I snapped and Mack hemmed me up more.

"Do Vinny know you fucking my nigga?" Kia asked and the girl rolled her eyes.

"Kia it ain't personal, and to be fair it's for the best. You got way more than enough to hold you over," the girl calmly spoke. I had to admit she carried herself as a boss too.

"So, let me inform you on some shit, bitch. Have fun now because Renzo is like a stray dog, he roams to anyone that's feeding him real good at the time. That nigga don't owe you loyalty! All he going to do is give you some wet pussy, while you're being used! I promise he will always take care of me and that's on your daddy bitch!" Kia gave the little exotic looking chick a piece of her mind. The girl stepped up closer to Kia, pushing Renzo slightly behind her.

"And give me a reason, Kia. You may be from the hood, but baby I run every corner of these streets, legally and illegally. So, let me make myself clear. Step in the arena with me you better be prepared to have an army with you, little girl," The chick tried to check my cousin, but after that it was game over. Kia calmly grabbed her bag, took out a wad of money and threw it on top of the table. She looked back at Yams who was getting up walking behind her. Kia walked past Renzo and stopped by the white chick and took the drink in her hand and held on to the cup while she threw the liquid in the chick's face. The brown color liquid dripped down her face, on her chest, and clothes. All of them looked in shock as the girl face turned into pure anger. Home girl look so mad as she dangled her hands that got wet too.

"Oops!" Kia shrugged her shoulders with a smile. "I bet you need your army now," Kia taunted. After that all hell broke loose. Kia and the girl started fighting and we were trying to separate the two but when Kia pulled her gun out on Renzo, we were all on pause.

"Kia, baby you gon shoot me?" Renzo said and the white bitch looked at him in disgust.

"Fuck you Renzo. When I say I don't ever in life want to see you again, I mean that shit on my dead grandma! I don't ever want to see you again. Keep your nigga on a leash because he roams a lot." She looked at the chick. Everyone was in the state of shock. The owner came out and Mack was talking to him to make sure he didn't call the police. The bodyguards were now standing in front of the white girl but left Renzo open for a bullet.

"Kia!" Renzo yelled out to her, but she was backing away slowly with Yams in her ear coaching her to leave with his hand rested on her hip. "Kia, so you leaving with that nigga?" Renzo yelled after Kia, but she was walking out the door.

I shook my head as I walk past the group behind Troy. Renzo looked at me in defeat. I was more so worried about myself because I was trying to sneak away from Mack's silly ass, but when that nigga yelled my name, I turned around in fear. I looked at Troy with the I'm sorry eyes, as he shook his head in defeat and kept walking. I knew I needed to be with my cousin but I wanted my man so I did what was best for me at the time and that was to stay, but I would soon find out that wasn't the best option for me.

FINDING MYSELF

Kia

"So, bitch let me get this straight. This nigga
got you locked up in the house with the bitch and
his daughter?" I asked Amber in disbelief. My
cousin was living some sister wives shit since this
nigga found her ass with Troy.

"Bitch, yes and I can't take it no more. This
bitch is purposely doing shit and he keeps telling
me I created the situation and until I DNA this fake
ass baby, I ain't leaving his sight. The nigga makes
me go with him to do runs and all. He thinks the
minute he leaves, I'm going to disappear, and shit.
The nigga ain't lying though because I am." Amber
complained, but I wasn't trying to hear the dumb
ass shit she was talking. It had been a month and I
told that dumb ass girl to come back home to me,
but she wanted to make sure Tina didn't sink her
claws into Mack. If you asked me, I swear they all
was fucking in that house because his daughter was

running around calling Amber mom and shit too. Shit was mad weird and crazy.

"Girl, please. You in that house enjoying the fact you got two niggas and a baby," I sucked on my mango I had in my hand while I lounged on the couch with Yams rubbing my feet,

"Bitch! Shut up!" Amber cackled. I knew there was some truth to what I was saying. She could lie all she wants to but ain't no bitch sleeping in a house with her niggas ex and his baby.

"No bitch you get the fuck up off the dick being dumb" I told her silly ass.

"Bitch I been trying to stay on the dick so I can have this fake ass baby," she whined, and I burst out laughing. I sometimes forgot that my cousin was real life carrying my burden of a secret.

"Well, look I'm planning on ending that ASAP, so I need you to get away from your Ménage Trois for a day, so you can go with me." I truthfully told her. I was over the pregnancy. I was sick of being sick and I was only like eight weeks. I didn't want to become further along and then be stuck with a baby.

"Damn, you sure about this Kia?" Amber sighed. I could tell she wanted me to keep the baby, but that was just not in my plans right now. I couldn't figure out what I wanted to do with my life. I had no job and no type of income. I thanked God for Yams because I was able to sit on my money longer, since he was eager to pay my damn bills.

"Positive, because I'm sick of eating just mangos because everything else makes me sick." I truthfully told her. I looked over at Yams who finally dozed off from rubbing my feet.

"Well, I will get in trouble for you so I will be there," she advised.

"Good, because Heaven coming too, y'all can finally really make-up," I told her, and she sucked her teeth.

"So, she can judge me? I think not," Amber refused.

"Bitch you need Heaven because right now, if Heaven was around, you would have bossed up on that nigga and left that house! It's no way I'm playing nice with my enemy, so my nigga won't fuck her. Either you retarded or she is fucking the both of y'all," I said giving my personal opinion of her silly ass drama.

"Whatever, Kia. You always got some shit to say. No one said nothing when you were a fool for Renzo," she tried to compare.

"Girl, you definitely tried it, but that ain't nothing to compare to. While you over there auditioning for *Love and Hip Hop* looking like Amina with Peter Gunz," I burst into laughter.

"Bitch, fuck you!" Amber yelled and disconnected the line in my face. I continued to laugh because Amber was a special kind of stupid with what she was doing. I heard a knock at my door, and I got up to answer it. To see Heaven at the door, I opened it quickly.

"Bitch!!!!!" Heaven squealed and gave me a big hug.

"Where you been at?" I asked her as she walked further into the house. She peeked in the living room seeing Yams knocked out she headed towards the kitchen area, with me in tow.

"Girl working my ass off. I have been nonstop going, and I really came to celebrate," she cheesed.

"What we are celebrating?" I asked her.

"I sold a house, but the thing is, it was over a half a million dollar so baby that commission check about to be looking nice!" she squealed with excitement. I admired Heaven's drive to be successful. This was something I wanted. Something to accomplish and be happy about it.

"I wish I could be as successful," I sighed leaning on the counter with my elbows. My cousin's eyes turned into pure sympathy.

"Kia, you can have this. You just have to figure out what makes you happy," she smiled at me.

"I'm not sure if I even know anymore." I truthfully spoke.

"Well Kia you been in school, but you keep changing your damn major." She tried to lecture me, but I cut her off.

"Stop it right there. I don't want to hear that shit Heaven. I just need you to be supportive for once, help me figure this shit out!" I was under enough aggravation and listening to Heaven do what she does best and that's lecture, I knew with my mouth and hers it would get ugly, so I needed to just nip it in the bud now.

"Fine, so what do you take enjoyment in?" Heaven asked and I wasn't too sure about it.

"I'm not sure. I just know I want to be my own boss!" I told her.

"Well, aren't you in school for accounting?" Heaven asked.

"Yes, but I'm good with numbers. I can break someone finances down in my sleep," I smiled. I had changed my major from Health Administration to Business Administration, then to accounting.

"Why won't you start like some type of business where you assist businesses with their finance and taxes? You can charge people to create a budget system and make sure their business taxes and finances are in order," Heaven stated. Listening to her made me think more about what I wanted to do. Yes, I would be a good accountant, but I wanted something that was a hobby that I enjoyed doing.

"Well, you will figure it out. Don't stress yourself. Finish up school and trust me your calling will come to you in a way you never seen it coming." Heaven said and I smiled.

"Thanks, cuz. See I like when you give this type of advice." I smiled.

"Now can you cook a bitch a meal?" we both burst into laughter.

"Girl, this demon seed I'm carrying won't allow me to even breathe without throwing up," I told her. She laughed shaking her head.

"Look, that's all a part of being a mom. Did you decide what you wanted to do?" she questioned me, as she aimlessly scrolled through her phone.

"I'm getting rid of it," I advised as I grabbed a bottle of water out of the fridge.

"Well honestly, I don't blame you. I couldn't imagine being pregnant right now. I'm in the beginning of my career working for an elite company. I got my first big sale. I don't have time being no family woman right now. Plus I enjoy having my me time." Heaven's selfish opinion made me think about my mother. It's weird that I haven't seen her, but I wished she was here.

My phone rang taking me out of my thoughts. Seeing it was Renzo made my heart pound out of my chest. I had mixed feelings about when I last saw him, and he has been calling me every day trying to talk. I'm not going to lie he was wearing me down. I wasn't sure if it was the hormones or not, but I tell you one thing, lately I could only think about him.

"He still trying?" Heaven asked, without even looking up from her phone. I frowned my face because I hated when she did that.

"You didn't even look at the phone," I said in confusion.

"Girl you don't have no friends, and I know you was talking to Amber before I got here because that's normally the time y'all talk. Yams in the living room so who else could it be?" She waived me off.

"Girl it's time for you to go," I said annoyed. She continued looking in her phone ignoring me.

"Girl I was leaving anyway. A bitch got shit to do." Heaven finished tapping the screen of her phone before she looked up at me and smirked. "Well at least the seed of the devil's spawn got you looking pretty," she laughed, and I rolled my eyes. Heaven thought she was a comedian at times.

"Girl get the hell out of my house!" I laughed pointing at the door. She wasn't lying though. I was glowing like crazy. I walked her to the door and made sure to lock it. I turned around and got back on the couch with Yams. My movement woke him up.

"Damn, I need to go lay down," he yawned. I admired his sexy lips, making me want to kiss him. Just when I was about to lean in, his phone rang.

"Yo," he said. "Nigga what?" He continued with irritation. He sat up and I could tell whatever he was being told had him hot.

"Nigga what hospital? I swear y'all niggas was supposed to be gone from that spot. Why y'all still there? Y'all was supposed to be gone since yesterday! If my nigga dies because of y'all! I swear, y'all gon feel me!" Yams snapped ending the call. I don't think I ever seen Yams this angry. He stood up and looked over at me.

"Kia, when the last time you dealt with Renzo?" He calmly asked me, but his eyes told me something else. It was the look of an ice-cold killer. I never seen Yams in action, but from what I heard, he was nothing to be played with.

"What's wrong Zeke?" I called him by his real name. He glared at me as if I only made the situation worst.

"Kia, I'm the one asking the fucking questions. Now do you still talk to that nigga?" He yelled, making me jump back.

"Look, I haven't talk to that nigga since we were at Uncut. He been calling me, but I haven't been answering his calls," I truthfully told him.

"I swear on everything I love that nigga gon have to see me. Troy's in the hospital and it got your niggas name written all over it!" He started grabbing his phone and shit off the coffee table.

"First of all, Yams I understand you're mad, but you need take that shit down a notch. What y'all niggas got going on in them streets ain't got shit to do with me! Now I'm sorry about Troy and I will gladly be by your side while we head to the hospital," I bluntly told him. He frowned his face making me feel like I said something way out of line.

"Kia, I don't give a fuck about what you talking about! Yo nigga gon have me hanging out a window! And you crying at his funeral! When it comes to my family, I don't play! And that's on

God!" He mugged me. He walked to the door with me right on his heels.

"Killing Renzo solves what exactly? Y'all niggas can't never just make fucking money. It's always a beef!" I yelled after him.

"Kia you pushing it, and unless you want to end up like him, I suggest you keep your fucking mouth closed!" He threatened.

"Nigga did you just threaten me?" I frowned my face up at him as if he smelled bad. "Nigga you got me fucked up! I does this street shit nigga!" I was riled up and ready to whoop ass. He looked at me and smirked.

"Pick your team Kia and pick it wisely!" Yams stated before he walked out of the door. I wasn't sure what he meant but I needed to get to Amber and find out who set this shit up. Soon as I saw Yams was gone, I grabbed my shoes and bag and left out of the house so quick. I hopped in my truck and hauled ass to where Amber was staying.

I pulled up to some townhomes that Amber silly ass moved into with Mack and his damn family. I couldn't believe these two women let this nigga fool they ass like this. I knocked on the door and Mack came to the door. When he saw it was me, he mugged me, but I didn't give a fuck.

"Nigga fix yo face. That shit is dead and you still holding my fucking cousin hostage in this sister wives bullshit!" I snapped as I walked inside.

"Yo Kia chill. We just got Maliyah to go to sleep," he tried to hush me, but I didn't have one ounce of care in the world.

"Look, I didn't think you was here, but since you are what the fuck did y'all fools do? Y'all shot Troy? Really like why the fuck y'all do that stupid shit?" I stared at Mack and his reaction told me he definitely knew what was going on.

"He did what?" Amber came from the kitchen looking at Mack as if he was crazy.

"What you care for?" Mack dropped his hands to the side looking like he was ready to beat Amber's ass.

"Yo y'all niggas started a war with niggas y'all don't know and on top of that, I deal with one of the niggas! Y'all gon have the nigga thinking I set him up! Like y'all trippin'." I expressed in frustration.

"Kia, that's not our problem anymore. You fucking that nigga not us, and they shouldn't have robbed us. They thought we wasn't coming and we did right before they moved they shit." He gave me a few of the details.

"Mack that's how y'all feel? We supposed to be family more than anything," I was hurt to say the least. "I would never put y'all in harm's way," I continued.

"Kia, the shit was supposed to be a robbery, but I saw that nigga and all I could think about was him kissing Amber and shit went left." He sighed deeply.

"Look, y'all need to fix this shit or be ready because I never seen Yams like this. I'm not calling y'all no suckas or no shit like that, but y'all need to be careful and know who y'all make enemies with. Y'all niggas forget y'all all bleed the same color red."

"Kia, I gave that pussy ass nigga a warning shot. He needs to stop acting like he intensive care, ol soft ass nigga," Mack frowned his face. This couldn't be real. I know damn well this nigga didn't say he gave a person a warning shot like a bullet hit in the wrong area can't kill someone.

"Mack you a right fool, and Amber y'all belong together. The fuck is you on," I told them, and Mack shrugged his shoulders as if it was normal.

"Don't fuck with my money or my bitch and I won't have to handle up," he shrugged walking away from me.

"Well nigga you put me in danger. What if that nigga act crazy and do some shit to me because of y'all," I yelled, forgetting about the toddler that was still sleeping.

"Ssshhhh!" They both turned around and said at the same time. My face immediately went to the *"Well excuse me"* look.

"Oh, y'all is crazy in this house! This shit ain't right Mack and you know it. Amber take your stupid ass home and let this nigga deal with his baby mama drama by himself. What the fuck you is a live in nanny and fuck machine? Renzo would have been six feet under if he thought I was sleeping in the house with his baby mama I hated. Who I set up and all! Shit is ridiculous!" I harshly whispered.

"The fuck you mean set me up?" Tina said standing behind me. Mack gave me the death stare and I knew I had said too much.

"Nothing. Go back in the room," Mack said and Tina shook her head no as she began to put the pieces together in her head.

"Nigga you got me in this house with this bitch and you knew she set me up! She set me up to lose you? My first fucking love? The father of my kids!" She yelled and the perplexed looked on all of us made us do a double take.

"Kids? The fuck is you talking about we only got one baby," this dumb ass nigga said. I shook my head because I knew I opened up a can of damn worms.

"Nigga I'm fucking pregnant. You round here raw dogging the both of us! And my stupid ass just sitting here wanting a piece of you so bad, I accepted this bullshit!" Tina yelled between tears. I looked over at Amber who looked like she got the wind knocked out of her, but something was definitely fishy about their story.

"Nigga you got me fucking you and your bitch and she set me up? This can't be fucking real! Bitch I swear if I wasn't pregnant, I would whoop your ass, but I'm keeping my baby so I can remind you every day how your dumb ass fell for the okie doke just like me, bitch!" Tina said storming off in the direction of the stairs.

I was so shocked, even though I knew it, I was still in shock to hear it. I looked at Amber as she grabbed some stuff from the couch. Mack looked at her with pleading eyes.

"Baby please, look I will make Tina get rid of it. We got a child on the way. I can't have you getting upset we both know this shit was going on."

"Mack don't touch me. I'm already embarrassed enough! This shit been going on for a month and I'm supposed to believe she got pregnant in a month when I made y'all use condoms during every encounter?" she calmly spoke. I could hear Mack swallow hard, that mean that nigga was in the pussy on PTO. Yep this some Jerry Springer shit here. I looked at both of them in complete disgust.

"Amber," he said, but the way she delivered a hard punch to his face and the way his head flew back, my cousin hit him hard as hell. She shook her hand because it was in pain and stormed off towards the front door.

"What about your clothes?" I questioned behind her.

"Fuck them clothes. I will buy new ones on this nigga tab!" She yelled back and I looked back at Mack and shook my head. *What in the entanglement is going on here?* I said to myself as we walked out the door. I don't think this shit could get any worst.

KNOWING HER WORTH

Renzo

I thought back to when we all stood in the middle of the warehouse. Mack was standing next to me. I looked at our small crew and was proud that they were the type of niggas that was always on go. The way we handled that shit with Yams gave me a different type of high. The money I lost, I got back and then some. I knew we would have to make changes for retaliation, but a nigga lived for this shit. I was not about to let no nigga try me and think I was a bitch nigga. If he thought he could run down on us and we were going to lay down, his mental was all fucked up. No nigga walking could ever say they got one up on me. Now I needed to get Kia off his dick, so I could take over his area and get my bitch back. This was my new plan of action. My thoughts were interrupted by the pretty exotic woman standing in front of me in a small maid outfit that barely covered prominent parts of her womanly body. She had all her body weight shifted on her right leg making her booty more visible from the front. Her stance demanded attention and she definitely had mine for the moment.

Lately she been on this dressing up shit and I was feeling it. Nadia did everything to keep a nigga wanting more but the problem was she wasn't Kia. Kia had the best part of me and that was my heart. I low key felt like Nadia knew it and that's why she didn't want me anywhere near Kia or her family. I laid my head back on the couch with a lit joint in between my fingers that I was already smoking. I watched her hit the play button on the stereo and the tunes of Teyanna Taylor's single *Morning*" played. The only reason I knew the song was because Kia liked it a lot. *Damn see what I mean she is everywhere in my head* I thought to myself. Nadia dropped down in a squat position with her legs opened wide. If you ask me, I swear this girl use to be a stripper. She began to seductively mouth the words to the song.

Ain't no limit what I'm pullin' when I fuck on you, babe

Oh no

Talk that shit, play with that clit and watch it
rain on you, baby
Funny how you thought out to the world we
was lookin'
We're just gettin' started, oh-whoa
Hit it, quit it
Fill that shit, get it
Make it, fuck it, feel it
Touch it, ooh (oh)
Titties in your mouth
With your tongue on it, whoa-oh

She glided her hands between her crotch slowly while she winded her hips. She was really seducing a nigga. I was solid as a rock once she was done winding her body all the way up and began to seductively walk closer to me. I got comfortable because I knew Nadia was ready to prove her point in this little show she was giving me. She began unzipping my pants as she looked at me with her eyes low and full of desire. I could tell she wanted it bad at this point. Her mouth watered for my erection. When she found what she was looking for, her eyes were full of excitement and the way she slowly kissed the head of my erection, she had my whole dick jumping. I was about to shove it in her mouth until she swallowed it whole making me moan like a bitch. Damn this girl's tonsils were the truth. She was working her throat muscles and tongue like my dick was the best thing to food. I wanted to hit the joint, but she had me stuck. The head was so good I don't think I could think of anything else. I was on the verge of about to burst when my phone started ringing. I looked down and could barely open my eyes good to see who it was. Hitting the ignore button, Nadia kept going like nothing was about to stop her from completing the task at hand. My phone rang again. This time I really opened my eyes to see who it was. Seeing it was Kia, the excitement made me burst a huge nut down Nadia's throat. She swallowed and looked up at me with a smile and wiped her mouth with the back of her hand. She was just about to get up, but she glanced at my ringing phone that I silenced.

"Are you fucking kidding me? Why the hell is she calling you?" Nadia stood up visibly upset.

"I'm not sure," I got up with my dick still at attention ready to body some pussy.

"What do you mean you're not sure? Renzo, I told you to leave her where she stands. She got a nigga already. Let that nigga have her!" she stated. "I don't know what you and Yams see in her anyway! She is ghetto with no fucking ambition," she continued with an insult. That little comment made my dick limp and I questioned how the fuck she knew the nigga Yams name, especially when I never told her.

"How do you know Yams?" I asked her calmly. I put my dick back into my pants and zipped them up. The mug I gave her made her take a step back.

"I don't know him. I just know because you mentioned him to me," she brushed it off, trying to walk by but I yanked her bright light ass back.

"Nadia, I don't give a fuck about who yo family is. You better start talking before I show you how I really get down," I said through clenched teeth. She rolled her eyes and snatched away from me.

"I know Yams because I'm his plug too," she folded her arms across her chest, and I slapped the shit out of her. Her faced turned beet red in embarrassment and from my hand hitting her skin.

"You got me out here doing all types of shit and you his fucking plug? Stop breaking the nigga off," I told her. She looked at me as if I was crazy.

"You're fucking crazy. I will not do that. He cops more dope than you ever did, until now. He has been with my family for years." She held her face, as her anger began to build up.

"Family? Who because Vinny never mentioned the nigga?" I questioned.

"My family, not Vinny's. Vinny never worked with him. And honestly you can't call shots since you still running around with Kia. You want your blocks to be yours? Drop Kia or I will put a bullet in her head and not think twice about!" she sneered before walking off.

"Man, I haven't been around her and you know it! Kia isn't the enemy. The nigga running down on your nigga investments is!" I snapped and she turned around looking at me.

"Fine, Renzo, but I will tell you this! I will do my part, but if I hear that Kia blew her breath in your direction, I'm going to make you watch me kill her, and that's on my dead mother!" she walked into the bedroom slamming the door. Not heading to her warning's, I text Kia back. I needed to know what she wanted. Soon as I hit the send button my phone rang and without looking because I thought it was Kia I answered.

"Yo,"

"Nigga, where you at I need you to slide through." Mack had been on ten since he shot Troy, but I think it was because he had all that drama between Amber and Tina.

"Nigga, the fuck you want?" I asked slightly annoyed.

"Man, I need you to see some shit because I want you to tell me if I'm trippin or not," he stated.

"I swear nigga you always got some weird shit going on. First you got a whole Ménage going on and now I got to come look at some weird shit. All I know if it's too off the wall, I'm kicking your ass for bothering me, yo!" I said before hanging up the phone. My phone chimed immediately in my hand. Seeing the "I need to talk to you" text, I immediately got excited. Kia wanted to talk so I was arranging a face to face meet up. I needed to see her in person without no one around. I text her back a meet up spot and after she agreed, I hurriedly went to take a shower. Nadia was in bed watching her T.V shows so I knew I had a good advantage to do me for a while before she started calling. Nadia was very needy and always wanted to know what a nigga was doing every five minutes. I swear she was getting crazier by the minute. Having me followed was enough to put me on guard when it came to her.

"Where are you going?" she started her normal line of questioning.

"Mack's," I simply said, and she nodded her head in agreement before looking back at the TV.

I quickly took a shower and got dressed making sure to put on everything that was Kia's favorite down to the shoes. Even though the crazy girl fucked up all my shit, I knew she loved to see a nigga in a Jordan set. Those gym shorts drove her ass nuts. I checked myself out in the mirror and sprayed her favorite cologne for me to wear. That Parfume de Marly Galloway made her ass drop them panties every time.

"Baby, can you bring me some Krispy Kreme doughnuts back please," she begged.

"Aight, I got you." I told her giving her kiss on the forehead. The genuine smile she wore made me feel bad that I was about to go against her. A niggas emotions were all over the place. Truth be told, a nigga should have never kicked it with her like I was single. It's crazy how I started a whole relationship while in one. I was real life living with someone other than Kia and honestly, it don't feel right.

Leaving my house and making my way to meet up with Kia, I was feeling a little nervous. We had not spoken since the incident at Uncut Miami. I was hoping that whatever she wanted to talk about, it was going to make me happy. Kia was known for being a natural buzz kill. I pulled up into the Wendy's parking lot near Miramar Parkway and University. Seeing her standing outside leaning on the truck I bought her, made me smile. She looked a little heavy but in all the right places. She had a natural glow about her. I parked my whip next to hers and she got inside my car. I had a joint already rolled ready to smoke one with her while we talked.

"So, what's on your mind?" I asked her and then lit the blunt.

"Look, why did you start that shit with Yams?" she asked me the dumbest question to man.

"That's what you wanted to talk about? Yo little ass nigga." I frowned my face. I hit the joint because I needed to calm down at this point.

"Renzo, you know I deal with him and you're putting me in the middle of y'all shit," She licked her full lips and pouted.

"I can't help it you wanted to fuck my enemy on some get back shit," I snapped.

"Nigga fuck you! I didn't fuck him on no get back nothing, I didn't even know y'all had fucking beef let alone even knew each other! And I know your ass ain't talking, while you over there fucking the plug and shit! You did that shit knowingly and had me sitting in that bitches face. Now it makes sense why her ass was so damn salty!" she frowned and folded her arms sitting back. Kia looked like a mad child that got reprimanded for bad behavior.

"What my shit got to do with what we talking about anyway? We talking about you trying to smooth some shit over for a fuck nigga? Why he got you handling his shit!" I tried to switch the topic from my indiscretions.

"You know what, you right. I thought by talking to you and tweetle dumb ass Mack, that y'all would understand that y'all put the so call women you once loved in some shit that could potentially put them in harm's way, but y'all so fucked up in the head it's all about your egos. What if Troy wanted to retaliate and shoot Amber or do some crazy shit to her? Or what if Yams say fuck that and put one in my dome, then what? Y'all niggas are so retarded and careless. I always told you if the money flowing, there is no need to start no shit that can jeopardize that. Who the fucks idea was it to get more traps anyway? Renzo this was supposed to be a come up, now you on some take out the competition type shit. You're not the same person." She shook her head like she was disappointed.

"Kia, you thought a nigga wanted to stop. That's your dream not mine. I want to get this money until I have so much, I'm going to need to bury the shit." I expressed.

"Or us burying you," her comment stung and set the mood for the silence that swept over in the car. "Look Renzo be careful. I don't know what Yams is planning but he is acting like I set him up, and I don't even know where your new traps are or his for that matter." She grabbed the handle of the door.

"Kia, listen I'm sorry,.I love and fuck with you heavy and I never want anything bad to happen to you and that's on everything I love man," I told her and she smiled weakly at me before getting out the car. I wanted to stop her and just hug her one time, but my pride wouldn't let me. I let the love of my life get away from me again.

Pulling up to Mack's house that he shared with Amber, I got out the car and made my way to the door and was just about to knock when the door swung open. He stood back so I could come in.

"Nigga, you were waiting at the window or some shit," I chuckled.

"Nigga you forgot this crazy ass girl got cameras everywhere these days." He said slamming and locking the door.

"Damn, nigga what's going on that you got me over here with your silly ass and where the hell is Amber?" I asked sitting down on the couch and grabbing the grinder to grind up my weed. I had been smoking heavy lately. Between all the shit I had going on this was my stress relief for the moment.

"Man, follow me," he said, making me get back up again. We walk in the master bedroom then to the bathroom. He opens the cabinet. I notice it has to be Amber side because of all the feminine stuff I saw.

"Am I trippin' bruh? I noticed all the damn pads and tampons shit is gone," Mack said with a confused look.

"Wait, but ain't she pregnant and ain't she supposed to be at your crib with Tina?" I asked even more lost.

"Man that part is a long story, but she back at Kia house. I came here because I saw her ass come here on the camera, but let me show you some shit," he said with his phone in his hand logging into the camera system. These damn people were weird with all these cameras inside of the house. I stared at the screen and my face immediately screwed up.

"Nigga is she taking the pads and shit?" I asked even more confused from the beginning.

"That's what I said," he was now hyped, because he felt like he caught some shit.

"Maybe she was giving them to Kia," I told him. As we watched Amber move around the house on the phone.

"No, this is what got me. Amber was supposed to setup her first doctor visit but she kept screaming it was too early, but I forced her to make an appointment, and you know now, they send text messages and email reminders. She hasn't gotten one from the doctor's office yet and her appointment is so called tomorrow but guess what? I found with an appointment card." He dug in his pocket pulling out a card for an abortion clinic with a tomorrow's date and time.

"Wait so Amber about to have an abortion?" I looked at him in shock.

"Exactly! That bitch is pregnant from that nigga and trying to get rid of it before I find out," he said a little too calm for my liking. Everyone knew Mack was all fun and games, until he became the silent killer.

"Nigga, what the hell you about to do?" Mad that I asked because I knew this fool was about to do something crazy.

"I'm going to the appointment too. She gone need someone to drive her ass to her grave after she been gutted out," this stupid nigga said like it was normal.

"Nigga you crazy as fuck," I fell out laughing walking back into the living room. I thought my life was crazy. Mack's ass had me beat.

"This shit ain't funny. Tina's ass pregnant again. Amber's ass carrying another niggas baby and lying about it. I can't make this shit up," he sat next to me on the couch grabbing the weed to roll him a joint.

"Well, at least you don't have her begging you to squash some beef. Kia wants a nigga to let that shit with Yams go," I told him lighting the blunt.

"Man, that nigga not going to stop. We shot his boy. That niggas mad and fired up," Mack stated as he rolled his joint and wet the wrap with it between his lips to help seal it.

"Man, I don't care what he does, but he ain't got no shooters like we do!" I was definitely sure of that. My niggas were always on go and never questioned a damn thing.

"Nigga, we can have all the shooters in the world, but if we don't move smart it makes everything we do pointless." Mack expressed his logic. I was hearing him loud and clear whether he knew it or not.

Once we had our joint's lit, we started planning our next move. I had found two replacement traps and moved the ones that was in Yams so call area. I decided to move it to Lil Haiti after getting confirmation that we were the only ones in this specific area in Lil Haiti. Little did anyone know, I had plans on taking Yams out. It

was between me and Chase. I only trusted Chase
with this because he was my shooter and we already
caught bodies together no one will ever know about.
I didn't like the feeling of having to constantly
looking over my shoulder. It's enough to deal with
envy as enemies but real-life people with pressure
made money slow, and that wasn't what I was on.

"So, we pulling up on that bitch tomorrow at
the clinic," Mack informed me, I just nodded my
head in agreement, because I had the smoke in my
mouth filling my lungs ready to release it.

"Yo, we need Sashay to run a shipment too.
I think tonight would be good too because it is
about to storm. You know ain't no lazy ass cop
stopping no cars in no thunderstorm." Mack said
and I had to nod my head in agreement to that.

"So, I will link with Chase, and have her go
to Key West and back." I told him before my phone
chimed. Seeing it was Nadia, I frowned my face.
She knew a nigga was working but she constantly
nagged even when I give her three days out the
week where I spent all my time with her.

"So, keep it a G. Who's worse her or Kia?"
Mack quizzed. I could tell he was definitely
interested in the answer.

"Honestly, I have to say Nadia, and that's
only because Kia and I did this shit together, so it
never seemed like she was nagging. The only time
Kia became a problem is when she was upset. It
seemed like I couldn't make her happy anymore." I
spoke the truth to my friend, who nodded his head
as he took a pull of the joint.

"Well, honestly. We made more money with
you being with Nadia, but you seemed more happier
when it was you and Kia. Now you have to figure
out is it worth losing your happiness." Mack was on
his shit today with the gems he was trying to drop
on me.

"So, you an expert now? Nigga why you
still playing with Tina? Who is it you love more
nigga?" I chuckled.

"I mean I love, well still in love with
Amber, but I'm not going to lie, with Tina being
pregnant, it just makes more since to just be with

her and raise our kids. I don't want another man around them and if I'm going to do that, then my happiness has to wait until my kids are older," Mack made a valid point. As a man I don't think I could handle that shit as well.

"Nigga, you gon have Amber fucked up. She already did some wild shit to separate you and Tina" I began to laugh, and he mugged me. "Tell the truth nigga you were fucking both of them, weren't you?" I continued while laughing and holding my stomach because the shit was just funny to me.

"Aight nigga, I see you a comedian, but on some real shit between you and me I was knocking both they ass down at the same time," He smirked and I fell back on the couch cracking up laughing.

"Nigga, I knew it! Ain't no nigga living with his BM and fiancé, and not having no ménage. How the hell you pulled that off when them hoes hate each other?" I curiously asked.

"Well, Tina is about that life. It was getting Amber's ass to loosen up. One night I had Amber on some weed brownies, alcohol, and her grown ass wanted to smoke on my joint too. She was so throwed we were sitting on the patio talking. I think she was in her feelings about the situation and just wanted me to talk to her, so she was just doing everything with a nigga. Tina got off work that night and came outside with us. Amber was so damn high she was sitting in front of me with her legs gapped open with one leg in my lap. Next thing I know Tina was down there licking the hell out of Amber's red pussy. I couldn't believe it. Amber was so far gone she could barely move let alone stop her. Shit, after watching for so long man I made Amber bend over on the chair while Tina licked her clit and played with my balls," Mack shrugged, and my mouth fell open in shock.

"Got damn it. Why I didn't do no shit like that with Kia's ass?" I frowned with an attitude realizing I was missing out on how real life was now.

"Nigga shut up. That shit is hell, because I swear at times, they were competing against each other and sometimes I thought they were in love with each other. Just fucking weird." Mack stated as he looked out in space not really focusing his eyes on anything. I swear he was imagining that the shit was happening right in front of him now.

"Nigga, now y'all is some different type of freaks. Y'all got freaklations going on. I don't think an entanglement got shit on what the hell y'all doing," I truthfully spoke. My friend and his love affair were way too much for a nigga like me, could ever deal with.

"You say that now until a bitch licking your balls while you're pounding some pussy," he bragged.

"You know what nigga that do sound good," I imagined how that shit would feel.

"Look at your ass just sitting there wishing you was me right now," Mack laughed but I laughed harder.

"Nigga, never. Your ass got a baby on the way with your baby mama and your fiancé might be pregnant from the nigga you watched her kiss on hidden cameras in y'all house!" I laughed harder. "Shit, I think my life maybe a little better nigga," I continued but I could tell Mack was not feeling me cracking on him and his relationship problems.

"Man fuck you!" he barked, and I burst into laughter again. This nigga could be mad all he wanted but his truth was funny as hell.

"Nigga don't get mad at me because your little triangle of a Ménage is messed up because Kia made Amber come to her senses."

"Man, I wanted to slap the shit out of Kia, but I knew her manly ass would have beat my ass along with Amber." He honestly spoke and I laughed harder. Everyone knew that Kia could box a nigga the hell up.

"Well, let me slide. I'm going to go holla at Sashay and then go home. What time are we pulling up on Amber?" I asked and he sat pondering for a few moments as he rubbed his chin.

"Her appointment is at 11 am but we need to be there when they show-up, so pull up at 10:30 and don't be late nigga," Mack grilled me.

"I got you nigga, damn!" I dapped him up and left his house. I needed to stop and grab this girl's doughnuts, but first, I needed to see Sashay. I pulled up to the A.P.T's and hopped out the car. I don't care what time I came around, this place always had someone outside. I walked down the breezeway until I made it to Sashay's front door. I knocked and her older sister answered, and she rolled her eyes at the sight of me. I mugged her ass back as she stood back to reluctantly let me in the house.

"Sashay! Someone's here for you!" she yelled out to her sister before walking down the hall of the small three bedroom apartment.

"Casey, why you didn't just say it was Renzo?" Sashay yelled after her older sister, as she rolled her eyes to the ceiling. "She's always doing the most," Sashay said as she approached me. I knew why her sister didn't like me and it was because she was mad I chose to fuck on and lace her younger sister and not her. Sashay's sister Casey was someone I would let suck my dick and keep it moving until I laid eyes on Sashay. Her younger sister was prettier and easier to deal with. I was real surprised that she never told her sister about me and her, but I think she was more embarrassed she got used and treated the way she did by me to ever speak on it.

"What you doing here though?" Sashay licked her full lips.

"I need you to make a run for me. It's about to storm and this would be the perfect time to go. I already got Chase ready on standby" I told her, and she nodded her head in agreement.

"Well, let me change my clothes and then we can slide." She said. I followed behind her to her room. I sat on her bed and looked around the room. I loved the fact that Sashay was OCD with her neatness. I watched her move around the room getting her stuff together. I noticed schoolbooks neatly stacked against the wall on the dresser.

"You never told a nigga what you in school for?" I asked her and she looked up at me while she leaned down looking in the drawer.

"Well. I decided to be a teacher," she proudly said, and I immediately laughed. Her face immediately frowned.

"It's not that, I mean a teacher? You like kids like that?" I asked.

"Well, I watch all my little cousins, nieces, and nephews. I'm always teaching them and realized they listen to me and love when I am teaching them new things." I could tell I made her feel bad.

"Look, I didn't mean to make you feel bad. I didn't know that about you. I always seen you watching them, but I thought you did it for money or some shit. I didn't know you took pride in keeping them." I tried to make her feel better about her decision.

"Well, I do. I have a schedule laid out for them when I do keep them, and they always are ahead when they start back school from the summer. I love kids and I think I would be great at it." She smiled as she put a shirt over her head.

"It's a good look, maybe one day you will run your own school," I told her, and I could tell she was in deep thought before she looked at me and smiled.

She was fully dressed, and she had a long-braided ponytail in her head that made all her features on her face standout. Sashay wasn't ugly and she didn't need to keep herself up to remain beautiful. To me her natural state just made her gorgeous. She was thick and had a little pudge from being pregnant and then losing the baby. Her newfound weight made her thick in all the right places. We left from her house and met up with Chase. After giving her the instructions on what she needed to do, I watched her drive away to get her trip started.

"You still knocking her down?" Chase curiously asked.

"Naw, actually. Why you want too?" I asked him and he frowned his face at me.

"Nigga I don't fuck behind homies. I was asking because she seems different. Her demeanor

has changed from what we have known for it to be."
He simply said. As we stood watching the car
disappear down the street.

"She's in school," I looked at Chase who
gave the same expression I gave when she told me,
which was a shocked one.

"Damn, she must have a new nigga or
something. You know hoes switch up for the right
nigga," he advised and there was definitely some
truth in that statement.

"I honestly told her ass that she needed to do
more with herself, but she wants to be a teacher."

"Well, that's a good look for her. She will
definitely have to change for kids, but I wonder how
she can handle that being the fact she lost her baby
fighting over you." Chase's comment stung as he
walked away and headed for his car. I never thought
about the damage of losing a child could do to
someone until now. My ringing phone took me out
of my thoughts. Seeing it was Nadia, I remembered
I needed to grab her doughnuts. Shaking my head
and silencing the phone, I went ahead and made my

way to get her doughnuts because I knew I couldn't be out any longer. These were the times I wished I was with Kia, but like they say the grass isn't always greener on the other side.

THE GAME HAS CHANGED

Kia

Amber, Heaven, and I sat at my dinner table. I watched as the two glared at each other not speaking. I was far from being annoyed. They had been beefing since our girls' trip that was ruined by our whack ass men. Amber had just got her hair done and was sporting a burgundy wig that was straight with a part down the middle. She had her nails long and lashes on full effect. Amber was the prissy cousin and always had to be slayed, while Heaven had to be classy and elegant in her words. Her nails were always short and always a nude or soft pink color. She had to always have neutral colors on her nails. Heaven wore her hair in a sew in that she rocked with light curls at the end. The hair stopped above her butt, but her stylist always had her hair blended so well people thought it was hers. The two were like night and day and as for me, I was just rough around the edges. My hair was pulled up in its normal bun. My real nails were manicured with a nude polish as well as my toes. I had on sweats as I sat at the table waiting for one of them to talk to each other. Heaven rolled her eyes at me, because she knew she would have to apologize first.

"Amber, I'm sorry about what happened. We are family, and we shouldn't act like that with each other." She sincerely said. Amber stared at her and I just knew she was about to say something slick.

"Bitch, I forgive you, but I swear on my momma, you do that shit again, I'm going to beat your ass senseless. You was dead ass wrong, but I love you and miss you, because being around Kia was driving me nuts. The girl don't fix herself up for nothing in the world," Amber complained but I didn't give a fuck. They weren't having morning sickness and had to go to school. I couldn't bear to sit through a lecture without feeling like I was dying. Heaven was laughing but it stopped the moment she looked at me.

"Kia are you ok? You don't look ok?"
Heaven looked concerned.

"That damn baby about to take her ass out,"
Amber shook her head without feeling one ounce of
sympathy.

"Heaven, I'm so glad this baby is coming
out. I need my life back," I complained. My
stomach was in knots and I felt like I was having a
case of the sweats.

"Kia, do you really want to do this?"
Heaven asked with concerned.

"Heaven leave her alone. The baby has to
go. Look at her. The girl is practically dying trying
to keep the little seed of Chuckie." Amber's mouth
could be so crazy at times.

"Bitch why is it the seed of Chuckie?"
Heaven cackled.

"Girl, have you seen the daddy?" Amber
shook her head with her nose scrunched up as if she
smelled something bad. We all laughed at that point
because we all knew Renzo was a whole hot mess
in these streets.

"Girl, don't toot your nose up at Kia, because I heard about your ass," Heaven said and it piqued my interest because I know for a fact I didn't tell this bitch nothing much, but that she was back living with me.

"Well, talk then. You know more than me?" Amber folded her arms as she glared at me.

"Girl, I didn't say nothing, but that you were living with me and wasn't staying with Mack's crazy ass anymore." I truthfully told her.

"Girl, everyone knows that you were living with Tina and Mack. That is not no secret," Heaven frowned at the fact that Amber was trying to be secretive.

"What you mean everyone knows?" Amber leaned forward on the table ready to hear Heaven spill how she was able to get details of her personal life without her telling it.

"Amber your living with your enemy, who is…if you ask me low key obsessed with your ass. You don't think she is going to run her mouth?"

Heaven said, but I knew Heaven very well, she was hiding something.

"No, I don't think she would say anything because it's fucking embarrassing, and for your F.Y.I, I live with Kia," Amber got up visibly upset at what Heaven knew. I knew ever since Heaven snitched on her back on our vacation, I knew Amber wouldn't trust her like that.

"Heaven, if she don't mention it just leave it alone ok," I advised her, but she rolled her eyes at me, annoyed at me taking Amber's side.

"Kia, she come for you but then don't never tell her shit. All I'm going to say is wait till the real tea get spilled. All I know is I want a front row seat to your facial expression when it does come up," Heaven leaned back in her seat and sipped the bottle water that sat in her hand.

"Well, until then leave it alone. Now let's go to my appointment." I told her, little did Heaven know I just found out, so nothing she said would surprise me at this point.

I had my only friends and family I trusted with my life come with me to make one of the hardest decisions I had to do in my life. I got up feeling lightheaded and praying once this baby was out of me, I could feel like myself again. I walked down the hallway to my room and grabbed my big MCM tote and knocked lightly on the room door that Amber was sleeping in. Amber swung the door open and her eyes were red like she been crying. This was nothing new. Since Amber been here, that's all she been doing. Since finding out that Tina was pregnant again, I knew that Amber was over Mack at this point. Well, at least that's what I was hoping because if she didn't know it, to see my cousin happy I would beat that damn baby out of Tina just like I did Sashay's ass. One thing about me, don't mess with my blood. I go hard for them because I knew at the end of the day, they went hard for me.

"Amber, you good? It's time to go," I looked at her with sympathetic eyes. Yep, it was official. I was going to beat the baby out that bitch, because Amber had always been the life of the party and the happiest person out of all of us.

"I'm ok, let me grab my purse," she walked back into the room and grabbed her purse off the bed that was decorated in a white comforter set, that had a vibrant yellow and silver pillows on it. Walking away back to the living room, I found Heaven in her phone for the first time ever smiling. The way I was able to see all thirty-two teeth in her mouth I knew it was not a damn client.

"Well, who the hell got you smiling like that?" I asked her and she jumped like she was caught. I eyed her suspiciously because that was not normal for her. Heaven was never the jumpy type and was always straight forward, never secretive.

"Girl, work email, my client was being funny," she quickly responded putting her phone in her bag and standing up from the couch.

"Hmmm hmmph," I rolled my eyes at her lies. Heaven lied too good, that's how you knew when she was lying. "Listen y'all two, make-up now because I'm not about to deal with y'all bullshit while I get sucked and prodded to get this baby out. I need y'all right now!" I got emotional as I walked out of my house slamming the door. I hit the locks on my truck and got in. I was emotional wreck. My phone chimed and seeing it was Yams. I got all types of anxiety because he had not been answering my calls or texts.

      Yammy: *Checking on you, will see u lata,*

      I smiled at the thought he still cared, but I was too mad that he been ignoring me. Hitting the side button, I locked my phone. I put my phone in my bag and waited for my cousins to come out of the house. It took them an additional ten minutes, but I didn't mind. I needed to mentally get myself together for what I was about to do. They got in the car and we rode in silence to the abortion clinic. I could tell they wanted to say something to me, but really didn't know what to say. My mind drifted to Renzo and how happy I knew he would have been about me being pregnant with his baby. I was still in love with Renzo, but I refused to let this nigga drag me in the mud because of different women or a dollar. Money and women was always a distraction for Renzo.

"So, we just gon act like we going to a funeral?" Amber said beginning to touch the radio and I slapped her hand.

"Ouch!" she yelled out.

"Girl, it is a funeral. The funeral of seed of Chuckie," Heaven stated without a care in the world.

"And you got on me for being mean to her and now you are agreeing with me. I can't wait till she is back to normal and not moody no more," Amber rolled her eyes directing her comment to Heaven.

"Fuck both of y'all," I spat, wishing I never told they ass to come with me in the first place. I was now aggravated and ready for this shit to be over with.

Pulling up to the grey building, I looked at the sign and the queasy feeling in my stomach came back. We all sat in the car in silence. It's like we were all about to do it, but it was just me by myself.

I was so used to my cousins going through every painful situation with me, but this here was a different type of feeling. I didn't feel connected to the baby yet, because I been making myself stay disconnected. I acted as if I wasn't pregnant, still doing my daily routines except when I was really sick with all day sickness, because it surely wasn't only morning sickness I was going through. I would be sick all day and night sometimes.

"C'mon let's go," I broke the silence opening my door. I headed towards the clinic and soon as I open the door, the smell of old mop water hit my nose. I saw a janitor wiping the already dirt stained floors with old mop water. Feeling my stomach turn into knots, I just knew this smell was going to bother me. I walked to the front desk and tapped on the little window.

"Hola, Mami. You have an appointment?" the lady's Spanish accent was strong as she wore a smile on her face.

"Yes," I simply said as she handed me the clip board.

"Feel dis out, and come back and I will get ju ready," she said. I swear in Miami everyone spoke Spanish or was Spanish. This place was indeed a melting pot. I walked back over to my cousins and sat in the middle of them and began to fill out the forms again. Reading over the paperwork, I realized I already did it. I got up and headed back to the window, I knocked and as soon as the window opened, I noticed this time someone else was there and she was much younger.

"Hello, I filled these papers out already," I advised her. I handed her the clipboard with all the papers on it.

"Sorry about that. What's your name?" the young girl asked.

"It's Kianna Grey," I told her and looked behind her at the other employees who looked to be doing everything but working. She tapped her long fingernails on the keyboard rapidly.

"There you are. I will let them know you're here and someone should be calling you soon," she informed me with a smile.

"Thank you," I told her and headed back to my seat. I observed the waiting room and for the first time ever I realized how many young girls were here. They all looked to be teenagers. I couldn't imagine being a mother now let alone a teen mom. There were faces of worry while others look to have been down this road before. After sitting for thirty minutes talking to my cousins, my name was called. I made my way to the back and as I walked down the hallway, I was beginning to have second thoughts. From the look of the place, it wasn't really a rundown place, but it surely wasn't my doctor's office over at Memorial Medical Center. The hallway had an old smell to it. The paint was chipped on the walls and around the doors. I noticed the equipment didn't look up to date as well. Everything in me screamed for me to leave, because one this place look like I was going to wake up without a baby and gain something else. The nurse showed me to my room and gave me instructions before she came back in to put me to sleep. I changed into the gown they provided and laid on the fake bed. I felt like I was just in here to do my routine gynecology visit. I got comfortable and closed my eyes and crossed my arms over my stomach for the first time. I don't know why but I felt emotional. The cold air made my nipples hard and made my body shiver. The door swung open.

"Hello, Ms. Grey, I'm Dr Rodriguez and I will be doing your procedure today, and my assistant Ms. Claribel will be giving you medicine to put you to sleep," She informed me. I nodded my head in agreement, but I never opened my eyes. I felt who I assumed to be Claribel, wrap the rubber band like material and tie it tight around my arm and prepared to insert the needle for the IV to put the medicine in it. All of a sudden, we heard shouting and screams. I kept my eyes closed wondering who was ghetto enough to cut up at the abortion clinic. I had my eyes still closed shut. When I heard the door swing open and a woman's voice yelled, "You cannot go in there!"

"Bitch! Shut the fuck up. If you don't want these problems you better back up!" he yelled.

Hearing Renzo's voice made my heart stop and my eyes to flutter open.

"You know what, you sittin here with yo legs cocked open for these damn women to see, trying to gut my baby out! This the fucking problem now. I let your ass go and you acting like a whole thot with your pussy on display. If you don't get yo ass up so I can pay these people for their troubles so they won't call nine on me!" his voice boomed in the small room. Scared shitless I couldn't even breath let alone move. I watch the doctor's sit in shock scared to move as well.

"Kia! Get yo ass up!" His voice boomed again vibrating against the walls of the small room making me jump up.

"Sir, she can't leave she has been heavily dosed with medication for the procedure." The nurse assistant Claribel said. I could tell from her shaky voice she was scared.

"Please, please just take the IV out. I'm so sorry" I begged her not wanting to fight. She nodded her head yes. She began removing the IV as fast as possible.

"Oh, now your ass is sorry. I can't believe your ass in here trying to gut my baby out and had us thinking hoeing ass Amber was gutting that nigga Troy's baby out of her!" he yelled at me.

"Nigga fuck you!" Amber yelled from down the hall. I then heard Mack yell at her, and they begin to argue. I was so embarrassed I was trying to grab my clothes.

"Oh! Your ass wants to be sneaky and shit. Sneak your ass right out this muthafucker in that damn flimsy hospital gown!" he shouted and all the color from my face faded.

"W-what? I can't go out there like this," I replied like a child.

"Kia you got five seconds and counting to put your clothes on before I drag your ass up out of here!" he advised. I was putting on my pants and before I could cover my ass good this nigga yelled five and dragged me straight up out of there. In the process, he dropped a knot of money at the front desk. I knew my ass ended up on World Star the way people had cameras out videotaping the madness. Heaven was yelling at Mack because he was man handling Amber while we were in the parking lot. It took us damn near twenty minutes to leave the parking lot.

I sat in the front seat of Renzo's whip barely able to keep my eyes open. The drugs were kicking in and I was soon to be sleep. I felt Renzo's glare periodically, but I wouldn't dare look his way. I just knew I was going to be free from my demon. He was like a damn leech and he was sucking me dry and now I knew he was going to be making sure I didn't go anywhere near a clinic. My phone rang making me look at the screen. Seeing Yams name flash across the screen, I leaned my head back in frustration. He was a good guy, but I knew we weren't going to make it because of Renzo.

"Don't ignore your nigga for me. I just want to make sure you and the nigga ain't hunching because if he poking his weak ass dick on my baby's head, I'm gon slap the shit out of you and kill him!" Renzo barked. I couldn't help but burst into laughter because Renzo was crazy as hell.

"Nigga what? The baby is fine. It's my vagina getting fucked, not the baby," I said and the sting to the face woke me the hell up.

"Kia, I would die about that muthafucker you carrying, so don't play me wit yo shit!" Renzo snapped. Suddenly tears came down my face and my feelings were completely hurt. We were toxic as fuck and I didn't want no parts in this anymore.

"Renzo, take me home now!" I cried.

"The hell you crying for? You brought this shit on yourself. Man fuck them alligator tears!" He yelled and I cried harder. He whipped the car into my driveway, and I tried to hurry up and get out of the car, but the medication was finally in full effect. I could barely make it around the car and to the door. Renzo was trying to help me, but I didn't want his help. I kept swatting his hands away as he tried to grab me. My car was coming up in the driveway behind Renzo's car and Heaven hopped out visibly annoyed. She walked up to me and Renzo.

"Nigga you hit my cousin?" Heaven snapped ready to fight, but me almost falling made them both not even try to argue anymore as Renzo picked me up and cradle me like a newborn baby. I closed my eyes and hearing the door open and the alarm go off, I felt relief as Renzo walked down the hall to my room. He laid me in the bed making sure to pull the covers back. He took my clothes off and then walked away. I could hear the water run in the bathtub.

"Is she ok?" Heaven asked.

"I think the meds she had in her arm is in her system. Can that harm the baby?" Renzo voice sounded scared.

"I'm not sure but we can make her a real doctor's appointment now and see if they will let her come first thing in the morning," Heaven told him.

"Aiight do that. She normally keeps all her doctor's information in her purple and pink notebook with the butterflies on it," I heard Renzo say. The fact he remembered had me in my feelings and I began to cry again. I couldn't make a sound because my body felt like dead weight, but the tears flowed down the side of my face.

"Ok, I will look for it," Heaven stated as I heard her going through my things. I didn't have the strength to move. I felt Renzo pick me up and walk me to the bathroom and put me in the tub.

"You smell like that place. You smell like death," he said beginning to wash me. I tried so hard to open my eyes, but at this point I needed to sleep the meds off, since I chose to be sedated and it was already flowing in my system, before Renzo showed up. The soothing warm water made me finally go into a deep sleep with the thoughts of Renzo's last words.

"Promise me you will never do that again.".

My eyes opened to my TV on the wall playing the movie *The Brothers*. I looked around and noticed it was dark. I heard laughter coming from my living room. I lifted my head up and realized I was laying on Renzo's chest. He had his hand behind his head with his mouth open knocked out. That only meant this nigga hadn't had no real sleep. I was slowly trying to get up as the thoughts of what happened in the clinic came back to me.

"I don't care what we go through. This was something I deserved to know. Please don't do that to me again," he pleaded.

"It's not going to happen, because this will be our one and only child together," I told him. I lifted off the bed and my growling stomach made Renzo sit up quickly.

"Lay down. I will go fix you something to eat. Heaven cooked. She made some soup and corn bread," he said getting off the bed. I nodded my head in agreement and laid back down and started watching the movie. I heard giggling and I saw Amber and Heaven at the door.

"Girl this is one for the books. Mack thought it was me until Renzo saw your bag in my lap," Amber told me. All I could do was shake my head.

"Girl, I never been so embarrassed," Heaven said while her hand was to her neck like she was clutching her pearls.

"Girl, Heaven's ass tried to act like she didn't know us, after sitting next to me. Girl I was screaming for his hoe while Mack tried to kill me for lying to him." Amber found humor in a bad situation.

"Listen, I was not about to be looked at as the ghetto people, or end up on World Star. The ghetto that went on in that place, them people about to ban our asses. I don't need my clients saying you was the girl in the abortion clinic fighting!" Heaven mocked in a squeaky voice sounding ratchet at the end of her spill. We all laughed because to see Heaven act like that was funny. We always known for her to be too bougie for everything.

"So, looks like we having a baby!" Amber squealed with excitement as they both came further in the room surrounding me and rubbing the belly that was nonexistent. All of sudden tears fell down my face.

"What's wrong?" Heaven asked with so much concern.

"I can't do this alone. Like Renzo is in a relationship with his damn boss. I don't think I can do this alone," I began to cry like a baby. I felt my cousin's wrap their arms around me to console me, but I knew I couldn't do this alone. I was always scared to get pregnant and always kept up with my pills, but I don't know how or even understand how this happened. God must have really wanted me to have this baby.

"Look if no one got you we definitely do!" Heaven said.

"On my life we got you cuz," Amber said and they both laid in bed hugging me as I cried. No matter what we went through my cousins were always there when I needed them.

BOSS MOVES

Nadia

The sun peeped through the window waking me up. Rubbing my eyes, I tried to lean up but feeling but the feeling of Renzo's heavy body wrapped around me stopped me. Reaching over to check my phone it was 7:30 in the morning. I needed to be in the office by nine this morning. Cleaning dirty money was one of the most important jobs in my family I had to do. The realty company I ran, helped me to do this, so well because we sold homes to our rich clients as well as middle class clients. We also did commercial properties as well. The business was lucrative and kept me busy just as much. I had to meet with a new employee who closed a deal on a half a million-dollar house in record timing. For her first time in the company, I noticed she had potential, but I never got to meet her face to face. Lightly pushing Renzo to the side, he rolled over to the other side of the bed. I got up and started my day. Going to the

155

kitchen fixing myself a cup of coffee, I noticed Renzo's phones on the counter. I walked past it, fighting with myself to not go through them. I started the coffee machine up so that I could brew me some coffee. I felt a yawn coming and yawned really big. I decided to make a quick healthy breakfast. After about twenty minutes. I had spinach and eggs, chicken sausage and wheat toast on a plate. I sat down at the kitchen counter with my cup of coffee and my laptop. I began to start going through emails and my list of clients. The buzzing of Renzo's phone made my eyes dart in that direction. Realizing the phone was flipped down I fought with myself to not look, but my gut was telling me to pick the phone up as it continued to vibrate on the counter. Turning the phone over the relief I felt when I saw Ricardo's name. I just knew for sure I was going to have to kill this man. One thing for sure I didn't play about my money nor my heart. Renzo didn't know what he had gotten himself into, but he surely would now. I heard

Renzo open the bedroom door, so I turned the phone back over on the counter.

"Why you up so early?" He yawned, and stretched his arms and wrapped them around shoulders, and began kissing me on the cheek.

"I have work this morning at the office. The newbie we hired sold a half a million-dollar house so I'm going to finally meet with her." I told him.

"Ok, well a nigga about to lay back down. I'm still sleepy," he complained and kissed my cheek one last time.

"Well what time you came into the house?" I questioned to see how long he was out.

"You know what I'm not sure. I was so high I never even looked at the time." He shrugged.

"Well chill on the weed. You don't want to ever get caught slipping. You need to be alert baby," I turned in the chair to face him pulling his arm towards me. His hand wrapped around my throat as he pulled me close to give me a deep kiss. If I didn't have to work, I would have put my man right back to sleep.

"I love you Renzo," I sweetly sang.

"I know you do," he aggressively pulled me closer to him as he kissed me again passionately.

For some reason this was unsettling to me. I knew I was in love with Renzo in this short period of time, but his feelings he could never express. I felt like in some crazy way he did love me, I mean why else would he stay with me and leave Kia? The self-doubt and questions were there but I would never show it. Renzo picked me up and sat me on the counter and explored my walls until I created the strongest waterfall between my legs. The passionate kisses turned into a whole quickie that had my legs shaking to the point when he let me down off the counter, I was wobbling. Sometimes are quickies could be so intense till it made me feel like he was in love with me but, that's was just a phase I refused to see.

After showering and putting on my clothes, I looked myself over in the floor length mirror admiring the black fitted skirt with the white blouse that exposed my cleavage, a simple diamond necklace laid on top of my bosoms. My hair was styled with a part down the middle with light curls in the end. I loved when my looks screamed Boss Status. I hurriedly grabbed my phone, keys, purse, and my laptop bag. I headed out the door quickly and realized Renzo didn't beg for me to stay even after our little quickie. Pushing my crazy thoughts to the side, I made my way to my car and drove through traffic. It took me about forty minutes to make it through Miami's morning traffic and that was good being the fact it was normally hours when going south of Miami. Arriving to my office, walking through the door and seeing my assistant running towards me with a cup from Starbucks.

"You made it. Here's your favorite Latte, and I have updated all meetings and you have some emails to get to. Also, don't forget you meet with our new employee."

"Breathe Kaylee," I said to her. I don't think she took a breath through her memo. As we walked into my private office, I turned and faced her; she wore a smile.

"Sorry boss, I like to make sure you're on point," my assistant Kaylee said. I smiled at her as she laid out my schedule. I had five realtors and just hired one more for my company. I needed the extra help since I had to tend to my uncle's business as well. I was overwhelmed and due for a vacation, a real one too. Not flying across the world to sell dope. I sat down in front of my desk but the confused look on Kaylee's face made me look side to side and then at her.

"Um, why are you looking at me like that?" I asked.

"I'm trying to understand why you are sitting and your meeting started five minutes ago with the new hire," she advised, and I jumped up quickly from my seat, feeling slightly embarrassed.

"You're right. Let me go," I hurriedly out of my office and to the room we had for meetings. I walked in and instantly looked at the beauty before me realizing something about her was so familiar.

"Hello, I'm Nadia." I extended my hand out.

"Hello, I'm Heaven," she stood up from her seat to greet me.

"Heaven, I heard you closed your first big deal after only being here for three weeks?"

"Yes, it's the love of ambition. I have already been doing this with another company for about three years. I have been getting my clientele up so that I can reach this level of success that I'm aiming for." She explained. For some reason she gave me a weird vibe, but I couldn't ignore her presence and drive.

"Listen, the fact you made that deal with little to no help, I will test you out with some of my elite clients." I told her.

"Really?" she said in shock.

"Listen you have a gift for selling. Everyone can't do that, and fortunately for you, I'm an impulse type of woman. I will just have my assistant oversee you during the visits with the clients. You make these sales and your commission will be bigger than your last." I told her. Her eyes brightened up at the thought.

"Wow, I'm speechless," she said.

"Listen my whole staff makes great money, but they all have earned it. If you want it too, you have to be dedicated to this and just put in the work. You will have clients call you all day sometimes but that's because they are spending substantial money." I advised. She nodded her head in agreement. I watched her soak in everything I told her. I knew she would be great asset to the team but something about her was so familiar that it was driving me crazy. I found myself staring at her quietly as she looked at me a little baffled.

"Um, do I go back to my desk?" She asked snapping me out of my thoughts.

"Yes of course. I'm sorry. I started thinking about something else and was distracted for a second." I lied. She smiled pleasantly and got up from her seat to leave.

My assistant came in and she looked at me and began laying out all my other important meetings. I was listening but I was trying to replay Heaven's face in my head over and over to figure out who she was. Kaylee gave me the rundown of clients waiting for responses and how many each of my realtors already had. As we took an hour to balance the clients per realtor, I had Kaylee to send out the client list to each realtor. This system we created helped each realtor to get an opportunity and also help us to keep the waiting clients moving. I had to create a system that allowed me to handle call backs and client wishes. We would get at least ten new clients every day. As she went back to her desk, I went in my office checking my messages on my phone. Seeing one message that stood out the most, I immediately grabbed my purse and headed towards the door. I stopped in front of Kaylee's desk.

"Kaylee, I have another meeting. Can you hold my calls please?" I advised her as I walked past her and headed towards the door, she nodded her head ok. I headed towards my car and got in.

I drove in and out of traffic toward the location that was in the message. When I pulled up to the white worn down warehouses, I became really nervous. Normally I always had someone with me but today I decided against it. Pulling my gun out of the glove compartment and placing it in the small of my back, I got out of the car. Staring at the black truck that look like midnight during the day. I saw the door open and Yams got out walking towards me. This man knew he looked good. Money definitely made him look even better. He walked towards me and his demeanor told me he was everything but happy. I waited for a response.

"So ya boy messing up my paper? Since you fucking him, he got you dick dumb?" His tone was everything but nice.

"Yams, what was our agreement?" I simply asked.

"What you want me to do if the nigga got a hold on her?" He stated.

"So, you don't have balls? You ain't a man?" I snapped.

"Yo you need to watch yo mouth! I can only do what the broad allow me to do. A nigga only came here to talk business. If you ain't supplying, I have to go with the competition and you know I will out do yo boy," Yams, cockily responded.

"So, you will go against us?" I questioned.

"Nadia, this ain't years ago. The only thing that moves and shakes is money. There is always someone with better numbers and product. The choice is yours. I'm always going to get money and if I was you, I would worry about the money and say fuck the love," he offered advice that I was barely interested in, but the fact he sounded like he knew something made me rethink my decision of asking.

"You want your product? Keep her busy until I get Renzo under control," I told him.

"And how do you expect to do that?" He asked.

"A bullet. So be sure she keeps seeing you, I will have the shipment delivered to you. I will reach out to you later with the time." I told him, and he smirked.

"Well, just so you know, ya boy got a mark on him, and I ain't playing fair. You know he ran

down on Troy!" He spat. I could tell he was getting
upset.

"Listen, I will deal with him and I will throw
in an extra on your shipment for the trouble but you
can't retaliate. He's already moved out of your
area," I tried to reason with him in this situation.

"I don't want yo extras. I want that nigga
and if I were you, I would be setting up his
funeral!" Yams finally said. His eyes were dark, and
he was very calm and firm in his position.

"Yams, like I said. Your extra will be in the
shipment and a hair on Renzo's head bet not be
touched. Go against me and that pretty pregnant
wife of yours will be dead," I firmly said getting in
my car, not caring about his eyes turning cold like
ice, or the pulsating vein in the side of his neck. I
knew one thing Yams better keep up his end of the
bargain, or things were about to get ugly.

I pulled off without even giving him a
second look. I don't know how men think they can
hide another family. Eventually the shit hits the fan
at some point. This man had a whole pregnant wife

at home but was chasing every skirt his eyes landed on. It was so easy to use this man to get to Kia. Once I figured out they were already in each other's radar, I just had Yams go a little harder at pursuing her, but now I could feel something was wrong and that even with Yams in the picture, I don't think I could put a wedge in between Kia and Renzo any longer. My uncle calling my phone took me out of my thoughts, as I press the green icon to answer the phone.

"Hello uncle Vinny," I sweetly answered.

"I need you to come in briefly," he responded quickly in his heavy accent and disconnected the line. Not sure what that was about, I rushed over to my uncle's because one thing for sure, he was never short with me. I dialed Renzo's and he picked up immediately.

"Hello," his voice came through the phone sounding dead sleep. I smiled at the fact he was having one of his days where he stayed home, while I was out and about busy.

"Baby, you still sleep?" I asked him. I could hear the T.V playing in the background.

"Yea, you good?" The sleep was definitely evident in his voice and at that point, I didn't even want to continue talking to him.

"Yea, I was checking on you, but I will let you sleep. I will be home later." I told him.

"Aight," his voice still sounding sleepy. I disconnected the call with a smile.

After about twenty minutes, I finally made it to my uncle's house. After coming through the driveway and getting out the car, I walked past the guards as they opened the door for me. Walking further inside, I saw my uncle's wife. Rolling my eyes, I tried to fix my attitude before I spoke, but I real life, didn't like Vinny's wife at all. She always had something to say when it came to Vinny and our family business. Always sticking her nose where it didn't belong. She sat in the chair reading a book, while some type of jazz music played in the background.

"Hello Nadia. Vinny's in the cellar waiting on you," she said never looking up from my book. She always had this attitude like I was beneath her and honestly if it wasn't for my uncle's money, she would be a bum ass bitch living in the projects, like she was before Vinny laid eyes on her ass in the strip club. She had her nerve always turning her nose up at me. I didn't even respond to her. I bent the corner and headed straight to the cellar. I loved how Vinny's house was made. Before he moved Lolita in, I use to spend days here, but now I barely visited. This was the first time I had ever been or stayed in his house this much. I finally made it to the door of his office that was tucked away in the cellar. I took a deep breath and turn the handle to the door. He looked up at me and I couldn't read his expression, which wasn't good. I walked further inside and closed the door behind me.

"You wanted to see me, Uncle Vinny?" I sweetly asked.

"Nadia, have a seat," he pointed to a chair that sat directly in front of him. I walked quickly and had a seat. "Nadia, I put you in this position because one, we are family. Two, you are dependable. Three, your understanding of respect of the family business. While I was away," he began to say, and he began to cough uncontrollably hard.

"Uncle Vinny are you ok?" I asked with concern. He nodded his head and cleared his throat. He sounded really bad.

"Something was brought to my attention. Renzo. I need you to stop seeing him on a personal level." He stated and at that point confusion was written all over my face. First of all, how did he even know that? "Don't look surprised. I know everything when it comes to family. You are mixing business and pleasure and the last time you did this. things went really bad; You left a mess that we had to clean up. I'm here to tell you Renzo is going to cause the same mess. I have known Renzo for a long time, and he has never left Kia alone for anyone. I need you to stay focused on the business or I will have to cut ties with you," He informed me. He tone was demanding with no room for arguing, but I was about to, whether he liked it or not.

"Vinny, no offense but he has left Kia. He is living with me now, and now we are a team. He has moved more weight than he ever did. He is moving all types of products; pills, weed, heroin, and coke. Business has not been affected based off our relationship. We even had arguments, and nothing has changed. He is still with me and we do live together. No disrespect Uncle, but I got this under control" I expressed in the most respectful way.

"Nadia, it's not your call when I have to clean up the shit when it gets ugly. Leave him alone and if you don't, I cannot help you when everything goes wrong." He advised, sitting back in his chair.

"Well, I guess you made your point," I said getting up.

"Mark my words Nadia. Nothing good is going to come from this, and I will not help you this time. Our family has too much to lose because of one person. I have talked to your father and I now see he is right. I and Lolita will be overseeing his business as well. You will continue to clean the money for now, but the minute I see any signs of trouble, we will move our money elsewhere." The fact that he mentioned my father's name I was pissed.

"So, you both blindsided me? After all I have done for you both!" I raised my voice jumping up from the chair. "I fucking risk my life for this fucking family every day and because you disagree with the person I'm fucking, you want to disown me? Like he carries more weight than I do!" I yelled. My anger was boiling over. I had enough of my family dictating every part of my life. Living under a crime family was always scary and a risk every time you walked out the door. From police to enemies.

"You need to calm down Nadia!" my uncle began to get upset and he started coughing uncontrollably again.

"No, I won't. I have done everything for y'all and this how you act towards me over someone I'm fucking and was selling your dope?

He is not your biggest fucking earner so what does it matter for!" I yelled. Crown came inside because he heard the commotion and so did his wife. Vinny continued to cough, but this time is sounded like it hurt because of the harshness of it.

"Vinny, baby are you ok? Nadia, you need to leave," Lolita demanded.

"I need to leave? He is my fucking blood," I snapped on her.

"Listen little girl. I let your antics slide all the time, but Vinny never told you why I became his wife, so if I were you, I would leave before yo ass writes a check you can't cash," Her bougie ass voice was gone and the project voice appeared just that quick. I frowned my face ready to snap, but the look on my Uncle's face as if he was losing oxygen made me stop. Crown pulled out his phone dialing 911. Lolita tried to her best to help him as I stood there and watched for what felt like hours. I was stuck. I loved my uncle and I didn't want the argument we were having to be the cause of his death.

"Nadia! Move out of the way!" Lolita screamed, as the paramedics tried to get by me. I finally allowed the tears to fall as Crown moved me out of the way. I didn't know this situation was going to be my saddest day, but also create the biggest change of my life.

BABY BLUES

Kia

    I sat quietly on the table playing with my fingers, as I waited for the doctor to come in. The room was silent. I could hear Renzo playing his phone, trying to keep his self-occupied. I Ever since yesterday with the chain of events that happened, I had not been able to call Yams to let him know anything. Renzo didn't leave my house until late and then he showed up at my house this morning. It felt weird being in his presence,.I felt so irritated because he didn't know, but when I was taking a shower, before the appointment, I heard him lie to Nadia, about being sleep. I honestly felt disgusted, because I knew if he did it to her he definitely did that shit to me. Ever since, my whole vibe has been thrown off. I heard a knock at the door before my nurse practitioner came in.

    "Hello, Ms. Grey. How are you feeling?" she warmly spoke, with a smile.

"Hello Donna. I'm ok I guess." I responded dryly.

"Well, I see you're here for your first prenatal visit? Don't seem so down. This a joyous moment," giving me her infectious smile again.

"You're right," I finally smiled back.

"Good, is this daddy?" she questioned.

"Yep, it's him. Renzo Ms. Donna is talking to you," I said loudly making him look in our direction.

"Oh, umm, my bad I was sending an important text. I'm all ears now." He said standing up placing the phone back in his back pocket. He walked closer to me and grabbed my hand. She smiled at him and started my exam. After doing my pelvic exam, making me pee on another pregnancy test, and doing blood work. It was finally time to hear the heartbeat. As she applied the cold jelly on my stomach. She moved the wand like object around my stomach while trying to pick up his heartbeat.

"Ahh! There it is," She said excitedly, followed by the strongest and rapidly beating heartbeat.

"Is that normal? I asked her, and she smiled warmly.

"Yes, it is, nice and strong. Listen, I'm going to give you a ton of brochures and a sheet of meds that are ok to take during different discomforts. The anesthesia won't do much harm to the baby, but we will keep an eye on you for the next two months to make sure the baby is developing good." She informed me as she wiped the gel off my stomach off.

"So does the morning sickness stop because I haven't been able to eat a thing," I whined.

"Well, try light foods first and if it gets worse, come seem me as soon as possible because without more nutrients, it can affect you and the baby." She explained. I nodded my head ok, as Reno's gently caressed the small of my back.

"So, for now, you parents are having a very healthy baby on the way. Oh! And please stay hydrated Kia," she added. I nodded my head in agreement. "Ok get dressed and go see the front desk for your next appointment," she advised, before she walked out of the room. I got up and began to get dress. Even though Renzo and I was not together, I was still comfortable enough to be naked in front of him.

"Damn your stomach so small," he said staring at me.

"I know right, but I gained weight everywhere else." I said to him as I got dressed.

"I see your ass getting fatter," as he tapped me on the ass making me laugh. I continued pulling my dress over my head until it was fully down. I don't think I will ever not feel comfortable around Renzo. I was so use to him seeing me naked, it was like second nature if I got dressed in front of him. I slipped on my sandals and grabbed my bag. I opened the door and we both walked out of the exam room and headed to the front desk for my next appointment. Renzo was being a totally different person. He held the door open, for me allowing me to walk into the hallway of Memorial Medical Center. He had his hand rested in the small of my back as he led me to the elevators. When we got to the valet booth, he gave the valet man the ticket and as we waited for the car, I noticed him staring at me.

"What?" I blushed.

"Nothing, just trying to see what has changed about you so far. Like you glowing and shit, but I really want to go through this shit with you Kia," he continued to admire me. I was speechless, because I just knew he wasn't into the whole pregnancy thing.

"Renzo, I don't mind you being here for your child, but you don't have to be a part of this pregnancy. I knew what I signed up for at this point..." I was cut off by the valet bringing the car back. We got back in the car and the whole ride to my house was quiet. The weird tension was so thick you couldn't cut it with a knife. It was way too thick for that. I wanted for me and Renzo to be in a good place for this baby that was growing inside of me.

We made it to my house, and before I could open my door good, Renzo was already at the passenger door opening it. I smiled, but I was starting to think this nigga thought I was fragile or something. I wasn't even showing, and he was acting like I was seven months pregnant. If its only been day two since he knew, I wonder how he is going to act the rest of the pregnancy. I walked to my door and used my keys to open the door, with Renzo right behind me. I walked into the house smelling like a home cooked meal. I walked further in to see my cousin's and Mack sitting in the living room. They were all laughing and when they laid eyes on me, my cousin's jumped up.

"Hey, what did the doctor say? Come sit down." Amber insisted.

"You hungry?" Heaven asked.

"Um, no I just need to sit down. I'm beginning to feel a little lightheaded." I told them. I didn't know how the hell I was going to make it through nine months of this bullshit.

"You want to lay in the room?" Renzo whispered in my ear with his hand in the small of my back. I nodded my head yes.

"I'm going to take her in the room to lay down. Heaven fix her some soup. I'm going to try and feed her something. She hasn't eaten since yesterday. Amber can you pick up all this shit off this paper for morning sickness for her anything you think she made need," he gave off orders and went in his pocket peeling $300 off the wad of money, handing it to her before ushering me down the hall. I knew I was ok, but soon as I stepped in the door it's like my body gave out. I felt my stomach reflex. I knew there was no way I could throw up nothing. I held my hand over my mouth.

"You ok?" Renzo face was full of concern. I nodded my head yes even though I knew that was a lie. Before, I could react my throat was being coated with my stomach acid, as I took off towards the bathroom and began throwing up at this point water. I started sweating like crazy. Renzo was behind me holding my hair rubbing my back as I continued to fill the toilet with the acids of my stomach. I couldn't go on like this. I just needed to be ok.

After thirty minutes of emptying my stomach, I was showered, teeth brushed, rubbed down and now lying in bed relaxing with Renzo cuddled up next to me. As much as I loved the attention he was giving me, I knew it was only for the moment, because he had to go home to his girlfriend. I sat in deep thought when my phone rung. Seeing it was Yams, I looked over and notice Renzo was still sleep. I picked up the line.

"Hey," I answered.

"Hey, so how did everything go?" Yams asked about the abortion that never happened. I never got to speak with him since I got the procedure.

"Um, I didn't do it," I told him and the pause on the line made me feel nervous. I honestly like Yams, and we had talks about the pregnancy, but I think because I was so adamant about getting rid of it, that he was really happy about it.

"Well, what happened?" he asked.

"Can we talk tomorrow in person about it?" I asked him.

"Um, how about I come over tonight and we can talk about it?" He asked. I contemplated my decision in my head because of Renzo, but I knew he would be long gone before Yams came over anyway.

"I will call you and let you know," I hoped he didn't try and debate me, but to my surprise he agreed.

"That's cool, just hit me and you know I will pull up," he seemed to be stressed. I could hear it in his voice. I wanted to ask him what was wrong, but I didn't want to sit on the phone with him any longer with a sleeping Renzo next to me.

"Ok, I will call you later," I told him, and he disconnected the line without saying bye, which was not like him. I put my phone on the nightstand and got back comfortable in the bed. Renzo turned his body towards me.

"Next time let that phone ring when I'm here," Renzo tried to put down on me. A frown spread across my face.

"Nigga, what? You got a whole girlfriend you can't be serious?" I stared down at him lying peacefully without a care in a world. Like what he told me was not out of line.

"Did I stutter," he simply said, and I sucked my teeth nudging him.

"No, but you should've because you don't run shit here. Renzo, like for real why are you here?" I asked getting frustrated. He was sending mix signals to me.

"Look chill, Kia you always over thinking shit. I wanted to make sure you were good before I left. I just don't have much to do and decided to nap, that is all. Now lay yo ass down!" He snapped. Sucking my teeth, I reluctantly laid down and closed my eyes. Finally, I drifted off into a deep sleep and didn't wake up until my cell phone started ringing back to back. Slowly sitting up in bed I looked over and notice Renzo was gone. I low-key was mad, but I needed to check my feelings at the door because it wasn't my place to even be getting mad about some shit that didn't concern me anymore. Looking at the phone noticing it was Yams, I picked up the line.

"Hey, what's up?" I yawned and proceeded to wipe the sleep from my eyes.

"I'm about to grab food you want something before I come?" He asked me as usual before he came over.

"I just want mangos," I sort of whined. That was all this baby would really allow me to keep down, besides Heaven's soup.

"Man, you always got me in a store for some shit that ain't in season. Look I will bring you soup instead," he said making my catch an instant attitude.

"Nigga I don't want that shit. Why you just can't listen and find me some mangos," I snapped.

"See, you lucky you with child right now," he retorted, but he could say whatever he wanted, he bet not walk in this house without a damn mango.

"Whatever, I'm waiting on you," was all I said before disconnecting my line letting it be known I wanted what I wanted. I got up and showered and brush my teeth. Once I was finished, I found myself scrolling through Instagram and seeing Renzo post a pic of him looking like he was in deep thought. My crazy ass examined the background so good I could see that he was at a woman's house, and the condo looked so damn familiar. I instantly became irritated. I picked up my phone and dialed him.

"You good?" He picked up on the first ring.

"No, the fuck I'm not! Renzo stay away from me; I can't handle the attention and then you're gone! You keep playing with my emotions and I can't handle it! I just need you to stop being so damn nice right now or I'm liable to do some nut shit!" I expressed.

"Damn, you miss daddy already! I will hit you when I'm on my way back," his toxic ass said and all I could do was smile. Like what the fuck was wrong with me? Was I just as toxic?

"Renzo, I mean it. I can't do this, and I won't," the defeat was evident in my voice.

"Kia, you got my jit. I'm not about to play with you!" I could tell he was getting angry.

"Nigga play with you? Nigga you been playing with me every chance you got! Like don't fucking play yourself. Nigga if you could I would have been the PS4, you played me so damn much, but keep fucking with me and watch what the fuck I do. I'm gon run these plays like Madden on your stupid ass!" I snapped.

"Man shut yo silly ass up. A nigga can't look out for a bitch before she thinks she is being wanted," he cut me off. For some reason it hurt my feelings to hear him say that. Insinuating that he didn't want me anymore. I looked at the phone in disbelief as I shook my head.

"Nigga fuck your stupid ass, I don't need you! What you better figure out if you really the daddy!" My impulse got the best of me. I knew it was definitely Renzo's baby, but my feelings were hurt.

"Oh, so you want a nigga to body ya nigga, aiight cool, bet!" He said and hung up in my face. My anger was on ten and I wanted to go find me a nigga because one thing I hated was to be hung up on. I stormed out of the room and down to the kitchen. Snatching the fridge door open to get some water.

"Well what's wrong with you?" Amber asked, while she sat at the island counter eating a bowl of cereal.

"Renzo's ass. Like nigga you playing, bothering me and you at a whole bitches house. I'm so mad we even laid in the bed together," I rolled my eyes, while opening the bottle of water.

"Kia what is your ass talking about? Y'all not together. He honestly can do what he wants," Amber shrugged making me glare at her.

"So, he can come over bathe a bitch, feed a bitch, rub my stomach, make sure he taking care of me then up and leave to be with the next bitch and it's ok? Yep, you got a bird brain Amber. That's why Mack's silly ass be trying you. You don't fuck shit up! See I fuck shit up! One thing for sure, a nigga gon feel me when it comes to my feelings! I don't play about my shit!" I was so angry and honestly, I did understand Ambers concept, but I think I was still hurt from finding out he was messing with Nadia. The nigga was plain shiesty.

"Listen, I get what you are saying but getting yourself worked up over a nigga that don't want to be here ain't making it better. Use the fuck out the nigga. He's making more bread, so make him spend that shit! Yams pay your bills but make Renzo catch a dent in his pockets. Bitch, ask for stupid shit for all I care, but make that nigga pay and watch you be happy with another nigga period!" Amber tried to put me on game. "See you kick ass and break shit. I spend that money. Girl I have Mack's bank cards. Everything I have spent been on him, and all he gon do is say *you good or I'm sorry* because that's what these niggas is. Sorry as fuck," Amber started to get angry. I could tell that last part was more for herself.

"Ok, but I'm tearing shit up and spending his money too," I said before walking out of the kitchen. Before I could make it in the room there was a knock at the door. I turned around and saw the smirk on Ambers face.

"So, which one that is," Amber chuckled. I rolled my eyes and went to the door. Seeing Yams got me excited. He was always clean and dressed down. He was too damn fine. He looked down at me and smiled.

"Damn you beautiful," he said making me blush. I let him in the house and closed and lock the door. Following behind him to the kitchen, Amber had this goofy ass look on her face.

"Hey new cousin in law," this crazy girl said.

"Hey Amber. You know my brother been trying to holla at you," Ambers face turned beet red.

"I didn't know he still wanted to fuck with me," she said in shock.

"I guess he see something in you that your nigga not seeing," he shrugged. I noticed her sit in deep thought. Sometimes you had to be careful of what you told Amber. She could turn low key crazy about things and overthink. The wheels in her brain was going at this point.

"Where is my mangos?" I looked at Yams, noticing he had bags in his hands, but none of them look like Publix, Wendy's or food fair bags.

"Chill, I got you some soup from La Granja," he said as if it was ok.

"So, Yams you think doing what you want instead of what I ask for from the jump is going to make me happy? You must be out of your mind. Who told you to show up here without my mangos?" I caught an instant attitude.

"Oh, nigga she been on a war path. Good luck," Amber stuck her nose in my damn business before she got up from the table.

"Don't you got a business to run?" I sassed.

"Yep, but um don't get mad at me cuz you didn't get what you want from neither of these niggas," Amber shrugged and walked away. I rolled my eyes ready to slap the shit out of her. I turned to Yams who shook his head at me.

"Yams, don't you dare give me that look. All I asked for was mangos and I get soup. The fuck am I supposed to do with that shit?" I expressed. Yams looked at me in disbelief.

"Kia, I didn't come over here to feed you. I brought the shit out of courtesy. I came over because you wanted to talk, so sit yo ass down and eat the damn soup because from the looks of it you still fucking pregnant and this nigga must be know the way Amber's talking." Yams low key snapped on me. I'm not gon lie it turned me on in a weird way. Like *yessss nigga check me!* I stared at him for a brief moment and sat down.

"Ok fine. You're right I'm still pregnant. I tried to do it, but the nigga came in there waving a gun and dragging my ass out." I truthfully told him, and Yams face frowned up immediately.

"The fuck he dragging you for? See Kia this shit here I ain't got time for. A nigga fuck with you heavy. I'm willing to raise jit as our own and be a family, but your baby daddy got serious attachment issues. The nigga think he owns you, and that's something you need to stop. I can't rock with this shit, because I'm telling you, the nigga got a death wish already and if I feel like he stepping on my toes even more, honestly I will act on all threats. Just know the nigga only breathing because of you. My nigga had bullets pulled up out of him," Yams exaggerated. I knew it was a lie because Mack said he only hit him once.

"So, what do you want me to do Yams? He is the father of my unborn child?" I seriously asked.

"If you got to ask then maybe you not sure about us," He stared me down with deep piercing eyes.

"If I wasn't then you wouldn't be here," I more so tried to convince myself. Honestly it felt good to have a nigga that was so into me for once.

"Then prove it. You got to show me baby. That's all a nigga saying. You got the nigga coming here and taking you to appointments and shit," he revealed that he been watching me. "Don't look shocked. What you thought I wasn't gon pull up after you left the clinic where you were supposed to get an abortion? Like a nigga fuck wit you heavy so of course I'm going to pull up after to check on you. That's the real nigga in me, but I see Mack in and out your house along with Renzo. Yeah not cool lil mama," he leaned back on the counter top waiting for a response and honestly I didn't have one.

"You're right, so what do you want me to do? My unborn child is his, what am I supposed to do?" Even though I understood him, I just felt like what could I do? Renzo had a mind of his own.

"Don't ask me that. You need to figure that out," his response was short and firm. I almost felt like he was giving me an ultimatum. Like I needed to choose between the two. Not just find a way to deal with the fact I was having a baby with someone else.

"I'm asking because I almost feel like you want me to say fuck him and let you be the father." The confusion on my face was evident. Yams came closer to me. I could tell from the way he was looking that what I said was definitely how he felt.

"I mean do what's best for you. I'm going to slide. I got some business to tend to. I will check on you later and slide back through," he said before kissing me on the forehead. I walked him out and honestly, I felt weird after closing my door. *This nigga really wants me to walk around here acting like he fathered my child,* I thought to myself. If my life couldn't get any weirder. I went back in the kitchen and decided to eat the stupid chicken soup he bought, and after finishing it just like I thought I was over the toilet throwing my life up. This could not be my life with this damn baby.

DEEP IN MY FEELINGS

Amber

With all the drama going on in our lives, I decided that we needed a much needed girls day. With Heaven working so much, Kia could barely keep food down and I was constantly working as well and trying to help Kia the best way I could, me dealing with my whack ass cry baby ass fiancée; I knew we all just needed to reset. I had just finished with going over driver schedules and was about to walk out of my office to go to lunch, when in stormed Mack looking like he was ready to fucking kill me.

"Amber, you must want a nigga to put you six feet fucking under," he snapped. Unsure of what he could possibly be mad about I just stood there with a blank face. "So, your silly ass ain't got shit to say to me?" he asked, like I was supposed to be able to read minds.

"Mack, what the fuck do you want? I don't even know what the hell you're even breathing hard about," I replied with annoyance. I walked around him heading out of the door of my office.

"The fuck you mean you don't know?" he questioned me again like I real life knew what his problem was now. The crazy part is I had not seen Mack since the day Kia was snatched up out the clinic and it has been a whole two months now. I couldn't understand what the problem could possibly be.

"Christie, hold all my calls for today. Also, make sure the drivers do not be late to no deliveries today. We had a bad week with delayed deliveries, and I don't like that. Stay on top of them for me please." I advised my assistant.

"Noted. I will make sure," she replied jotting notes down.

"Also, can you please review payroll for me to be sure it's ready to go for ADP by the end of today so that checks can go out this Friday," I reminded her.

"Already done, boss," she advised with a smile. Christie loved when she completed a task before I even asked. She took pride in her job. That's why I loved her.

"Good, oh and forward all calls to Mack since he is breathing down my neck," I rolled my eyes and she giggled. This was normal for her to see Mack come in the office fussing or hearing me go off on him about something. I walked out the door of our building with Mack hot on my heels. "Damn, Mack just tell me what the fuck the damn problem is so you can leave me the fuck alone.

"Amber, the fact you acting clueless is going to make me strangle your ass. What the fuck you needed fifty bands for? The fuck you taking money out my stash for?" he snapped. At that point I laughed so hard, because this whole time, I thought this nigga really had something interesting to be mad about.

"Nigga, the fuck you mean? I took it because one I wanted to and two, I'm getting me my own shit," I revealed.

"Amber, you got two houses the fuck you mean you need a place to stay? Ain't you staying with Kia?" his stupid response made me laugh again.

"Mack, you must be out of your rabbit ass mind if for one I'm staying in the house with you and Tina again, and two the other place was our home together, but since I'm moving on, being independent is the goal, but it's on your dime since you made it this way!" I snapped. I leaned on one leg as I shook the other because I was irritated. I took the money to get me a nice little condo. Just wait till he found out how much I took out our joint accounts to cover a year's mortgage and to renovate the place. He was about to kill me if he was stressing over $50,000.

"Amber, you don't need a new fucking place. What you want it for anyways so you can go and be a hoe? What you want to fuck on niggas?" he barked. At this point he had people turning around staring at us like we were a good soap opera.

"Maybe, shit Tina's on baby number two. I thought I could work on baby number…" I was cut off by his wrapped around my throat.

"Bitch, I'll kill you," Mack growled in my ear. The way my pussy got wet, I just knew my silly ass was crazy. The murderous stare turned me the hell on. I bit my lip as he stared down at me. The sly smirk came after letting me know he knew what I was thinking.

"As mad as I am, only you would like this crazy ass shit," He tongued me down on the sidewalk. "I'm gon let you have this independent freedom, but the minute I feel like a nigga dreaming about your pussy, I'm going to be sure that you and that nigga going to be in the grave." He continued. I backed up slightly because I knew I was going to be slick. I needed to gain control over the situation because my pussy sometimes had a mind of its own.

"Mack, do me a favor. Go buy your new baby some pampers and leave me the fuck alone. We are done! I don't care what my pussy is talking right now, but it definitely won't be you," I began to walk away and head to my car.

"Amber, your pussy better talk M, A, C and muthafucking K!" he shouted at me.

"Nigga the only language my pussy talk is your fucking bank account numbers nigga!" I said before hitting the locks on my car door and getting inside. Mack didn't know it yet, but he lost me. I couldn't deal with another baby. I loved him with all my heart, but our relationship was officially over, and I was ready to start a new life all on his dime too. I was a firm believer a nigga causes you pain make his ass pay literally. I purposely turned on City Girls *Pussy Talk* and drove past that nigga sticking my middle finger at his ass while he stood there looking dumb.

I know what I did was probably messed the hell up, but when I loved someone, I loved hard and Tina was in the way, plain and simple. I don't know how I allowed Mack to get me into letting this bitch lick my pussy from the front to the back, but I loved him so much I was willing to do anything to keep him around, but that baby shit made all that shit go out the window. Especially when the couple of times we did do a ménage, I made the nigga strap up. The nigga had to be tapping the bottom of Tina's pussy raw when I wasn't around or before the little arrangement we had going on. I knew that I needed my cousin's because I needed them to remind me the type of bitch I was. I was not no *Love and Hip Hop* scandal type of bitch. Like this nigga have really fucked my head up in the worst way. I pulled up to Eden Roc Hotel and valeted my car. I made it to the lobby of the SPA, and I saw Heaven and Kia sitting down talking. As soon as they noticed me, they stood up and hugged me. Kia looked like she was losing too much weight to be pregnant and Heaven had a damn glow.

"Kia are you ok?" I was completely concerned for my cousin. She had an upcoming appointment, and I hoped the doctor could fix her morning sickness.

"Girl good as it will get with seed of Chuckie," she simply said, but she definitely wasn't looking to good.

"Poor baby," Heaven babied her, as she rubbed her back.

"Well, you're glowing so what's tea?" I said to her and she just smiled.

"Oh, hell no. What she keeping," I looked at Kia because I knew she knew what it was. They had been around each other more since I been working more. Now, Heaven's schedule wasn't as strict as mine, she was able to check on Kia more than me.

"Listen all I'm gon say is she finally getting dicked down," Kia tried to be hype when she said it, but I could tell it was hard because she wasn't looking good."

"Girl I will give y'all details later. Let's go. We were waiting on you before we started services," she urged as she started walking to the front desk. I had to admit whoever it was, this nigga was slanging pipe. Her whole walk had changed. I looked at Kia who giggled because she noticed it too. We followed behind her and once we were checked in and given our robes to change in, the relaxation began. I was enjoying the beautiful décor. The light oak wood, white and soft color greens provided a calming effect. The modern furniture was comforting. I was enjoying the tranquility this place was giving me already. We were all doing a treatment bath and I couldn't wait. Then after we were doing massages. We were escorted to the treatment bath and had we got comfortable and situated that's when we started to dive in our daily dose of dramas in our lives.

"So, let me get this straight. You haven't heard from Renzo since you told him to leave you alone?" Heaven quizzed. I was puzzled my damn self. Renzo made a promise to be there for Kia, but I haven't seen him around lately.

"Yep, the nigga finally respects my wishes, and me and Yams have been inseparable. Girl the nigga probably calling and texting me now going crazy." Kia shook her head with a sly smile.

"Seems like you're really into him," Heaven responded to Kia.

"I mean he is a great person like he pays for everything and makes sure I'm ok every day. He buys me flowers and always sending me sweet texts. What I like about him the most is that he talks to me with a plan. Like everything he says is like what we will do in the future. You know like he has plans for us and the baby, but something in me is telling me it is too good to be true," Kia expressed her feelings about Yams. It was refreshing to hear her talk happily about someone.

"Like I'm super happy for you. I noticed he been there more than ever lately," I responded.

"I mean I need help and your ass been working nonstop lately. I'm starting to think you're hiding something," she caught an attitude and sucked her teeth.

"Girl stop it. I'm working. Nothing to stress over. I got to make sure this baby straight because it's parents is retarded." I spoke as I leaned my head back in on the tub.

"I fucked Ricardo!" Heaven blurted out of nowhere. The way the both of our heads snapped in her direction.

"Bitch! What?" Me and Kia said in union.

"You heard me!" Heaven said without a smirk or anything.

"Oh hell no that nigga damn sure ain't got no 401k plan," Kia yelled out.

"Girl I just want to know was the dick good?" I truthfully asked, and my cousin's fell out laughing. I didn't care about nothing else. My cousin needed a real nigga to knock the bottom out of her pussy.

"OMG! Your mouth Amber," Kia laughed harder, but she looked like she was in pain.

"Well, we just be fucking. Nothing serious. I don't want a relationship with him, plus I'm back talking to Caleb," she slipped the last part in. I swear the vomit came up to my throat.

"Caleb?" Frowned.

"Yes and look I don't want to hear shit. He has changed and been going to therapy," she tried to convince herself more than us. Caleb was this L seven nigga who Heaven was engaged to, but the nigga used to beat all the sense out of her brain. The crazy part we always thought they had the perfect relationship until he broke her damn collar bone and causing her to have a damn concussion that put her stupid ass in a coma. If it wasn't for an old friend at the hospital to let us know, we would have never known the fool pushed her down the fucking stairs after whooping her ass. So, while she was in a coma, we tried to put him in one too. We went to that house and beat his ass with the help of Renzo. We tried to give his ass the same bruises and broken bones she had. Like niggas kill me. You beating on a bitch like you lost your mind. The crazy part is Heaven was way different back then. She was so sweet on a nigga she was in love with. Her strength came from leaving his stupid ass, but to go back I have to disagree.

"If that nigga ain't ready to die, tell him don't even play fight with you because if you think I carry my hammer for my health, you're sadly mistaken," Kia coldly said. Even in sickness this girl was still gutta. I loved her to death, but I could see why Renzo cheated sometimes. She couldn't just act like a damn lady. She was always ready to pop shit.

"Heaven, you looking for a legit nigga, but Ricardo might just change your mind, because the nigga loaded and he got legit business. He just a shoota," I shrugged, voicing my opinion.

"Girl, it's just sex. I'm good. I can't grow old with a drug dealer. I will leave that to y'all," she tried again to convince her damn self, but I knew if Ricardo started to really like her she was going to cause Caleb to die.

"Ok girl it's yo life," I expressed meaning every word, but I swear that nigga touch her again I was going to let Kia body the nigga this time around.

We continued our spa day relaxing and enjoying all the hotel perks. We decided to eat in the restaurant since it started raining and the air was becoming cool. I swear it was that time of the year in Miami where you were unsure whether to bring out the boots or bathing suits. Sitting at the restaurant table, we had already ordered our food but looking at Kia, she seemed like she wanted to pass the hell out. She was wiping her forehead from the beads of sweat forming.

"Kia, you sure you ok?" I asked her again, and she just nodded her head.

"It's this fucking devil I'm carrying. It's got to be a damn boy because he wants me to suffer like his daddy want me to suffer," she whimpered.

"When is your appointment?" I questioned her.

"Maybe you should move the appointment up Kia. You really don't look so good," Heaven chimed in.

"I think I just need to finally lay down." She took one more last deep breath before she tilted over on the floor and passed out. We screamed jumping up from the table, I ran over to Kia, lifting her head up trying to see if she was still breathing.

"Heaven, she is not breathing," I screamed as the tears started to fall. "Please someone help! Help!" I frantically yelled out. I cradled Kia as if she was a baby. I could hear Heaven yelling into the phone with the 911 operator.

"Amber you got to let her go. I need to perform CPR, or she is going to die," I finally heard Heaven as she tried to pry Kia away from me. It was all so fast from there, as I hovered over Heaven performing CPR with the help of a hotel worker. Hearing Kia cough made me so happy. I silently thanking God. Heaven got back on the phone with 911 letting them know she is breathing but her heartbeat was faint. I was just happy that she had a chance to fight for her life. It seemed like paramedics were right on time and went to work poking and prodding her. I could hear her whimper.

"Amber, I need you to get yourself together. Call Yams and meet us at the hospital. I have Caleb coming to grab my car. Listen Amber she is going to be fine, but I need you to get it together like now, because if you don't, we can't help her ok," she tried to talk some sense into me. I nodded my head up and down.

"Grab our bags, go find Yams and meet us at Mount Sinai," she told me. I could tell Heaven was trying to be level-headed and strong because she knew how I felt about them. I was the one ready to die with them all the time.

I grabbed all of our stuff, dropping more than what was needed for the food on the table and jogged out of the building and to valet. Letting the man know my sister is the one being taken out and to the hospital, he made me priority to get my car before anyone elses. Once I was in the car, I called the one person I knew who would know where Yams at.

"Damn you miss a nigga already? You just left me your relaxation day is over," he answered the phone being sarcastic as always.

"Baby," I sniffed as the tears fell down my eyes.

"What's wrong yo?" his voice became concerned.

"It's Kia. She is headed to the hospital. Can you please tell Yams to meet us at Mount Sinai?" I tried to quickly get it out before I started my crying shit again.

"Yo, just calm down Amber. Let me call bro now," he quickly said and put me on hold. After about three minutes he was back on the line.

"He said he on his way there now. Amber bae, I need you to calm down and breathe. Kia is strong. She will be ok," He tried to give me some comforting words.

"Thank you, Troy, I will see you later." I told him as I drove in and out of traffic trying to make it to the hospital.

"Aiight, call me when you're leaving," he responded.

"Ok," I told him and disconnected the line. I continued my drive for ten more minutes before I pulled up to the hospital. I parked and made my way to the lobby. After getting my picture taken and given a hospital sticker, I made my way to sit down. Because she just came in and they didn't even have her fully registered in the system yet. I called Heaven to see if she could help me get to her, but her phone went straight to voicemail. Getting frustrated I threw the phone in my bag and crossed my arms over my chest.

"Amber, is she ok?" Yams appeared out of nowhere. I had my head down, but I surely knew he did not come from outside because I was next to the door and would have heard them open and felt the wind. I looked at him suspiciously.

"I just came from the bathroom. I had been calling Heaven, but I got no answer," he said and his demeanor for the first time ever was off. This nigga gave me a sneaky vibe.

"Look, I'm not sure what's going on..." my ringing phone cut me off. I looked through my bag quickly until I found it. Seeing it was Heaven, I quickly answered.

"Hello, where are y'all?" I immediately asked. I eyed Yams suspiciously because something was off about him and then on top of that, I could have sworn I notice the hospital sticker he had on said an earlier time, but he turned around quickly the minute he saw me paying attention to it. Something was definitely off about this nigga and I couldn't wait to tell Kia when she woke up.

"Amber, did you hear the room number?" Heaven yelled in my ear again.

"Yes, Yams here too. We coming up," I said to her.

"Wait he got here quick as fuck?" she said what I had been thinking the whole time.

"Yea, I said the same thing, but we on our way up," I told her before disconnecting the line. I didn't want to discuss the sneaky nigga no more. I wanted to go see my cousin.

Yams followed me to my cousin's room. It took us a few minutes to even find it but when we did, she was laid out in the room, hooked on all types of machines and I could hear a loud beating noise sounding like a heartbeat.

"Hey, ssshhhh we have to keep her as calm as possible" Heaven whispered to us.

"Well, what's wrong with her?" I asked with extreme concern.

"For some reason, the girl is malnourished. The doctor said she is completely starving and that her throat is raw from throwing up so much. Did you two notice her still not being able to keep food down?" Heaven asked Yams and I. We both shook our heads no. "The doctor said he will be back once her labs come back in so he can review them and go over them with her." Heaven continued to whisper. I noticed Yams walk over to Kia's bed side and held her hand and rubbed her forehead before planting a kiss. As skeptical as I was of him, he did drop everything when it came to be by her side.

"I think she will be ok though. She kind of out of it. She is extremely fatigued." Heaven continued.

"This baby is killing her at this point," I spoke what I believed.

"Heaven," Kia could barely speak. Heaven quickly walked over to her bedside and I followed to. Kia looked bad. In a sense she looked sick, but her beauty always outshined that. Her curly tresses were now back black, and it was all over her head.

"What happened?" she began to wipe her eyes as she tried to sit up in the bed.

"Kia just relax," Yams softly told her.

"Kia you passed out at dinner. Do you remember that?" Heaven asked her.

"No I just remember sitting there feeling so tired." She explained.

"Well you're fine. I think they are going to keep you. Kia you know your body is not getting any nutrients. They were asking were you starving yourself.," Heaven informed her. Kia looked so lost like she didn't know what the heck Heaven was talking about.

"Well I eat but I'm always throwing up, and my throat has been killing me," she complained.

"Well they did some tests. Once it comes back they can let you know what's really wrong but on the good side seed of Chuckie's heartbeat is strong. Listen to it," Heaven lightly chuckled.

"You scared us," I finally spoke.

"Yea man I was here visiting my grandma when I got the call," Yams said. Even though it explained everything I still felt like he was lying.

"Damn, I'm sorry y'all. I guess I'm not as tough as I think I am. I was trying to just finally enjoy a day out," her voice was shaky and hard to listen to. It sounded bad.

"Just relax, because you scared us for the first twenty minutes in this place, they were poking you and doing all types of shit to you," Heaven gently grabbed her hand. More nurses came back in the room.

"She's up! Good! That means the IV with nutrients is giving her some strength back. Listen the doctor will come talk to her later to explain what's going on, but for now she will be admitted and won't be going home until she can keep solid foods down. Ms. Grey nod your head if you understand." Kia nodded her head yes.

The nurse went to work changing her IV bags and readjusting the band on her small pudge of a stomach. I never even realized Kia had lost so much weight. This is crazy her baby was sucking her dry like how Bella's baby did in Twilight. She had a little vampire in her damn stomach. Since she lost so much weight, you could notice the small pudge, but it was so small it looks like she was just bloated. I felt bad for her at this point. I wanted her to terminate the pregnancy because in reality what could you possibly be doing it for now since the nigga don't even want to be in a relationship. Renzo just wanted control, just like his fucking friend. I was so sick of these niggas at this point. I watched the nurse move about some more before she left out. I was beyond worried for her. I touched her hand, and she turned her head towards me. Kia's skin looked drained her lips were chap and she looked worn out.

"Kia, maybe you should terminate the pregnancy. Like this shit ain't normal. Look at you," I spoke. Her face frowned up. I could tell she wanted to say something, but she sighed deeply and I watched the tears roll down the side of her face.

"Amber, why the fuck would you even tell her that?" Heaven snapped.

"Well, what we supposes to watch the seed of Chuckie take her ass out? Look at her! She looks fucking helpless," I pointed at Kia, who laid there just staring at the wall.

"Amber, it's her choice. She is doing this for her unborn, and she will be fine. Women go through worst to bring their child in the world. Everyone is not selfish!" she yelled. Oh, this bitch was trying it on one of her motor mouths moment.

"Watch yourself Heaven. I live with Kia and see what the fuck it does to her," I rolled my neck pointing my finger at her.

"Bitch please, you been too busy sniffing up some niggas ass, because since you been dropping the ball, Yams and I have been taking care of her for the past two months. So, if she wants this fucking baby, she will keep it!" Heaven got in my face and that shit set me off more.

"She don't want this fucking baby! Renzo wants this fucking baby and the shit is fucking killing her! Like let's be real here. She was this close to doing it, but changed her fucking mind!" I knew I spoke too much once I seen Yams' face. He looked disappointed.

"But I got fucking loose lips? Bitch fuck you and go be a good sister wife to Mack and his baby mama," she scoffed and walked over to Kia who was visibly upset with me. I knew I shouldn't have spoken, but I was tired of seeing my cousin go through the worst pregnancy ever and the nigga was nowhere to be fucking found. Nobody has seen the nigga since he took her ass to her first appointment two months ago. Shit, I don't think he even called to check on her.

"Look, I'm going to step out. You want me to bring you anything?" Yams asked Kia.

"Ice, my throat is killing me," she complained. He nodded his head yes, giving her kiss on the forehead before he walked out the door.

"So, what you haven't been eating?" Heaven questioned her.

"I mean I was eating the soups and stuff, but I would throw it up. I told Yams two days ago I needed mangos because that was the only thing that would stay down, but he insisted on me to keep trying the soups because he didn't want me to get like diabetes or some shit because of all the sugar the mangos hold. So, I tried it his way, I ate the soups he brought and what you would cook, but I would always throw it up, so I haven't eaten since I threw up two days ago." She struggled to get everything out with her throat being sore.

"Well hopefully with you being in here they can get you to keep solid foods down," Heaven spoke.

"I'm sorry Kia. I didn't mean to say what I said with Yams being in the room," I truthfully told her. She nodded her head in understanding and then smiled.

"I mean, he will be ok. He's the one wanted to stay fucking with me, so no big deal," she reassured me. I could never take me and Kia beefing. We were the closest and she helped me with all my shenanigans.

"Do you work tonight?" Heaven asked sarcastically. I stuck my middle finger at her and was about to snap, when in walked in Renzo, Mack, Chase and Ricardo. My mood went from bad to worse. I was completely annoyed because no one called them.

"Like for real how did you even find her or knew?" Heaven looked puzzled the same way as me.

"A nigga never gives up their sources," Renzo stated.

"Nigga you a whole stalker. First you found her house now this? You a different type of crazy," I told him. Mack glared at me. I'm guessing he was still mad about earlier. I watched Renzo walk over to Kia, who laid helpless in the bed.

"Kia, what's wrong?" You could hear the concern in Renzo's voice. I knew he loved my cousin, he just was not good for her.

"Amber, you still trying my dawg," Chase walked up to me and gave me a hug.

"Tell your dawg stop roaming the streets and getting attached to fleas," I seriously spoke, and Chase cracked up laughing, only infuriating Mack. I noticed Ricardo was eyeing Heaven, who tried to act like she was in her phone. Renzo continued to talk to Kia and rub her forehead the same way Yams was doing earlier, how ironic.

"Damn, Kia yo ass look bad as fuck. What is that demon doing to you?" Chase blurted out loudly making Renzo glare at him. "Nigga the fuck you lookin at me like that for? Kia told you it wasn't your demon seed," Chase stated making us all look at Kia and Renzo as if they were crazy. The door opened and I instantly smirked at the sight of Caleb's big goofy ass walking through the hospital room door. The way all the niggas looked at him, had me laughing.

"Baby, I came to bring your keys," Caleb said looking around before his eyes landed on Renzo. I could tell he became antsy and annoyed.

He hated Renzo, but he surely couldn't beat him. "Renzo," he nodded his head and Renzo mugged him back without a word, making the other men in the room feel like Caleb was the damn enemy. Caleb didn't care about any of them when his eyes was on Heaven. He walked over and kissed her, making sure to grope her backside. He put the keys in her hand and kissed her again. I could tell Ricardo was feeling some type of way because he became antsy and walked out in frustration. If I didn't know any better, Heaven was lying about what was really going on with her and Ricardo. The way he watched her and Caleb interact, the pulsating vein on the side of his neck and head that nigga was 38 hot with her ass.

"I will see you later," Caleb kissed her again. It was like the nigga was proving his point and marking his territory in front of all of us. "Get well, Kia," he said dryly knowing Kia would never respond because we couldn't stand his ass. He walked out of the room door and the room went into an uproar.

"Heaven you really fucking with that lame ass nigga again?" Mack started it first.

"Mack, mind your business," She retorted.

"Naw, for real Heaven. That nigga put you in the hospital for days and you took his bitch ass back? That's whack as fuck," Renzo voiced his opinion and for the first time ever, he made sense.

"The nigga did what?" Ricardo asked looking like he was getting irritated.

"Man, that nigga use to beat the shit out of Heaven," Chase advised Ricardo who looked at Heaven in disgust.

"Really, Chase! Mind your damn business!" Heaven snapped.

"Nigga, I'm just speaking facts. Your ass should be ashamed, still messing with a nigga whose a bitch," Chase frowned his face not caring how Heaven felt. I watch Ricardo scoff and snatch the room door open walking out. Everyone looked in his direction confused, but Kia, I and Heaven knew his problem.

"What's wrong with that girly ass nigga?" Chase chuckled.

"Chase shut up. Your ass been running your mouth since you been here," Mack snapped before he stood directly in front of me. Trying to move around him, the doctor walked in drawing our attention to her.

"Hello, Everyone I'm Dr. Donna, and I'm Kia's OB/GYN." She introduced herself. We all spoke back in union saying "Hi".

"Well, Kia your results are back, and I noticed you're not getting any nutrients, which is not good. You have a serious case of HG which is Hyperemesis Gravidarum. You're unable to keep anything down to provide the proper nutrients to your child. This can cause the constant nausea and vomiting, and the weight loss. It also can make you very weak and have you passing out. So, to be sure you and the baby are stronger I'm going to admit you. You will be here until you can keep solid food other than mangos down," She smiled down at Kia who offered a slight smile in return. "Also, I will try some ice to help with the rawness of your throat. Once we can get you to stop vomiting, then your throat soreness should clear up. Any questions for me right now?" The doctor asked and Kia shook her head no. "I'm glad you have a huge support system because you're going to need them through your toughest days. If you need anything ring for your nurse on duty, and if it is serious, they will page me ok?" she reassured her. Kia nodded her ahead in agreement. "Bye everyone," she waved at everyone before she left. I noticed Renzo get in the bed with Kia while Chase and Heaven had their chairs pulled up close to Kia's bedside.

"So, we going to keep this shit up?" Mack said, I rolled my eyed about to walk away and he grabbed my arm, pulling me back to him.

"Mack, don't you have another child on the way? Figure that shit out over there because I'm not dealing with another child." I honestly told him. I was not about to play step mommy for another child.

"Amber, you tripping. Especially the shit you done pull. I'm not good enough for some shit you honestly know what was going on?" The statement Mack made, had me looking like he was Bozo the clown, because he had to be one to think I was that stupid to allow his ass to have another baby, and we were engaged.

"I know you got to be lacing your weed with something, because nigga do you hear yourself! I'm not playing step mammy to nan child that is after Maliyah!" I shouted and shoved his ass out of my way.

I had to get away from Mack, because I hated his presence. I know I did some shit but this type of pain of watching the same girl be able to do something that I didn't have the courage to do was unbearable. I got rid of me and Mack's baby a while ago because I couldn't be a mother. I felt like I wasn't ready and now after so many times of us having unprotected sex and Mack hard down giving me the nut, I couldn't get pregnant. I have spoken to doctors who told me the scar tissue from my abortion was bad and would cause me to miscarry, and that was about it, but I couldn't even get the damn eggs and sperm to damn meet. I think this was God's punishment for not being an honest person. I walked out of the room, pacing in the hallway trying to calm down, when I saw Ricardo down the hall walking back in my direction. Once he got closer, I realized how much him, and Renzo favored each other. Ricardo was the same complexion, but he had dreads, which was definitely different for Heaven. He was tall and he looked like he worked out. He had a mouth full of damn diamonds. Yep this nigga was about to turn Heaven's nine to five ass out. I smirked at him.

"What's so funny?" his baritone voice responded.

"Man listen, I know about you and Heaven," I honestly told him. He coolly looked at me.

"I don't know what you talkin' about Ambs." He nicknamed me that ever since I met him.

"Listen, if you want Heaven, you need to put down on her or she is going to handle you how she wants," I tried to offer him a little bit of advice. He smirked and nodded his head before he walked back inside Kia's hospital room with me in tow. Walking closer to my cousin, I touched her hand as she laid in the bed with Renzo. I wished he would get his act together because my cousin's heart was truly his.

"Kia, I will come back later to visit." She could barely keep her eyes open. She nodded her head yes. I walked over to Heaven, who was trying her best to seem occupied in her phone.

"I will be back later," I said, and she nodded her head yes not wanting to look at me. I walked out of the hospital room with Mack right on my heels. We argued all the way to valet. I was becoming so annoyed with him.

"You just don't get it, so let me help you. Let me go fuck a nigga and get pregnant and see how you feel about it later!" I yelled making everyone look at me.

"Amber don't make me do something silly bout you," Mack tried his best to control his anger around these white folks, but I knew he was about to explode. One thing for sure he hated to be embarrassed.

"Go focus on your baby mama with the two babies." My car pulled up just in time for me to hop in and watch how Mack's frustration and stress wore on his face. Maybe in another lifetime but this one right here I was done. I was not about to play the fool for no man.

I drove off and headed to my destination. It took me about another twenty minutes to get there. I was super excited about seeing him. I needed this breath of fresh air. I walked through the lobby and up the elevator after checking in. I finally made it to his room, and he was looking rough, but the happiness on his face said it all.

"Damn, I didn't think you would make it with Kia being sick," he said sitting on the bed.

"Troy, I told you I got you," I expressed.

231

"Well, a nigga wasn't sure being that you flake on me so much," he cracked.

"Ok, now don't get beat up too," I laughed. The nurse had a wheelchair ready for him. I walked over and helped him into the wheelchair. Mack said it was a warning shot, but the shit almost took the nigga out. I made sure before we left that I had all his belongings before I rolled him out of the hospital. It was crazy how we started to kick it more. Once I found out about him being in the hospital, I had to check on him. I was sure I would run into his fiancé, but that never happened, and he never spoke on her. I had my car parked to the side for easy access with all the traffic at Jackson Hospital. I finally was able to get him in with the help of the nurse, who looked like she was going to miss him terribly.

"Let me find out you and that damn nurse had a thing. She was too sad to see you gone," I sassed.

"Man, she was cool peoples. She just looked after a nigga. Plus she's married," he rubbed his beard with a smile. Troy was handsome, but he looked so young for his age. He was a mocha complexion, with the prettiest set of straight teeth, his eyes were dark and mysterious. His demeanor made him even more enticing. His hair was curly and wild, and needed to be cut again.

"I see. Well, where is your fiancé then?" I seriously wanted to know. He walked right into the question. He shook his head wearing a smirk.

"Shit, she in the driver seat, if she acts right," He tried to be slick.

"Oh, don't you dare try it." I laughed. "For real, what happened to her?" I asked more determined to know. He sighed deeply.

"She broke up with me the day I got shot. What's crazy is she never even asked if I was ok or nothing. She just left me and that was it. All those years and she didn't care if I lived or died," he looked out the window in deep thought. Regretting I ever brought up, but now it made sense why he tried to avoid the question or the situation. No one wants to feel that type of pain. I reached over and grabbed his hand.

"Listen, even if we never be together, you will always have me as a friend. I promise!" I held his hand strong and he kissed the back of it.

I drove him to his house where I would be helping him. I decided to stay with him for a little while to help him out until he healed fully. Once I got him comfortable on the couch, I began cleaning his place up. The fact it was fairly clean and just needed to be dusted. I could tell this wasn't the place he laid his head at with his ex, but I could tell she had been here a lot. I politely put all her belongings in a box and sat it by the front door. He lived in a townhouse. It was a nice community as well.

I decided to whip him up a quick meal. Making chili and rice along with cornbread. Comfort foods always made me happy and I wanted him to be happy and comfortable. Finally placing the food on a tray and bringing it to him on the couch. He smiled big.

"Looks like to me you belong here," he smiled. He tried to sit up and winced in pain.

"Let me help you," I grabbed his arm allowing him to get some pressure off his wound in back hip and leg. Mack failed to tell the truth that he shot this man more than once. Once he was situated, I pulled the tray closer to him. He looked in awe at the food.

"You sure you know how to cook?" he asked, and I laughed.

"Well, I can do a little something something. I learned from Heaven because my mama acted like her recipes were secrets," I rolled my eyes and he laughed, before taking a spoon full of food.

"Well, this ain't bad," he said in between chewing.

"Boy, don't talk with your mouth full," I popped him on his arm.

"Damn, I might have to keep you. A nigga hasn't had a home cooked meal in a while," he said.

"Well, that's weird. Sis didn't cook for you?" I asked and he shook his head no. Yep, I was done hearing about her, ain't no way I would let this man starve.

I found myself with Troy for the rest of the day. We talked about everything under the sun. He was really a good listener and had become a good friend. He has helped me to see things in a different light when it came to me and Mack. I loved the fact he didn't hate or give bad advice but offered good solid advice and how it could possibly help me and Mack. The fact he was ok with being just a friend if it came down to it, made me like him even more. I enjoyed every minute around him. When he would be my shoulder to cry on when he would come to my house where I lived at with Mack, I missed it and to be around him on a different level gave me butterflies. I was so comfortable around him it was crazy. We were laid up on the couch sleep when I felt the buzzing of his phone. I reached for it and seeing who it was made me cringe. Wishing I never grabbed it, I tapped him lightly letting him know he got a call. I didn't think he would answer the phone because I was there.

"Yo," he sounded annoyed. You could hear her yelling through the phone, but I was trying my best to mind my business.

"Ma, what you thought a nigga was going to pay all your shit after you left me knowing I got shot? Girl you crazy as fuck," he barked in the phone. I was annoyed he was even speaking to her but again, I was trying a different approach when it came to niggas, allowing them to choose, but Lord I wanted to curse homegirl out. You left your nigga for dead. Like be for real now.

"Look, a nigga is not helping you. I don't care what you talkin about," He continued, and you could tell she was reading him for filth the way she was screaming in the phone.

"Well, I guess it's time to get yo bread up and find you another rich nigga," he finally said before disconnecting the call. I watched him turn the phone completely off. "My bad," he simply said.

"You good. I ain't worried about it, but you could have paid that damn girl's rent so she can stop bothering you," I chucked.

"She better go get it how she lives, because the day she left me in the hospital sis was cut off. Can't help it that she allowed someone else to do her job," he mumbled with his eyes closed. I admired his long lashes and kissed his cheek. Damn, just like that I was starting to fall for Mr. Troy Adams.

TRYING AIN'T WORKING NO MORE

Mack

I was playing with my daughter as she ran around making car noises acting like she was driving. I finally came back to the home me and Amber shared. I noticed she had moved all her things out, so it was just me and my daughter. Tina and I finally talked, and we agreed co-parenting were our best option. She felt like I took Amber's side more even with all the new revelations of her sneakiness. Honestly, I didn't care because I loved Amber. They say when a nigga really loves a woman nothing can make them want to leave them. I was addicted to everything about Amber. She was the best part of me. She helped build our business, put me in the right direction. Honestly because of her she the reason why I went so hard to make sure everything she ever wanted happened for her. I knew she was burning a hole in money because she was mad, and at this point I didn't care, I watched her charge my accounts everyday with her expenses. I knew what she ate for breakfast down to her Walgreens charges. I guess I didn't care because she was still going to work like nothing happened making sure the business ran smoothly. I even noticing her doing some deliveries because some of the workers had called out. She was a determined woman and I think that's what I enjoyed the most about her.

"Dahddy!" Maliyah yelled taking me out of my thoughts. "Dahddy, Mama here," she happily sang. Not realizing I was so deep in thought I never heard the door open. I knew Maliyah was referring to Amber, because that's what she called her.

"Hi, princess Liyah," Amber picked her up showering her with hugs and kisses. Amber had grown to love Maliyah. Well maybe I forced it on her when we were all living in the house together.

"You never showed up to the office. We need to go over the books. I need to get these numbers and figures right for tax purposes. You know the season is coming up." Amber got straight to business.

"Yea, I been stuck babysitting," I honestly told her.

"Well, she needs to be in school. You have a business to run, and plus you act like Maliyah is super bad. You could have brought her into the office." She got me together really quick.

"You right. Let's handle this," I told her, and she pulled the books out of her big Louie bag and we got down to work.

It took us about an hour and a half to get everything fully worked out and balanced. She was able to find a way to squeeze more drug money into the business. When I say Kia taught her well on how to do this shit, Amber had everything looking legit to every last penny. I appreciated her for still handling up. Maliyah was sleep on a pallet on the floor near us. I watched Amber put everything back in her bag and stand up ready to leave. I walked her towards the door, but watching her fine slim ass made my dick jump. She had her hair done courtesy of me, because I saw when her ass bought the damn wig and paid the girl with my damn card. Amber's hair was wavy like and she had her long nails on and mink lashes in looking like damn snack. She turned around and all I saw was her full lips. Damn, I missed this girl. She had on a dress that was snugged against her skin. I could tell she put on a little weight. Must be from getting rid of me. You know what they say, women boss up and glow up after a bad relationship.

"So, I will see you in the office tomorrow because we need an extra driver, since one is out on vacation," she said but I was too mesmerized to respond. I grabbed her arm pulling her towards me and placing my lips on hers. She damn near melted in my arms. I could feel the rhythm of her heartbeat against my chest.

"Mack, I don't think this is a good idea," She pulled back slightly as she her chest went up and down heavily. "Mack please," she began to beg, but I wasn't hearing no I missed her. She only dealt with me when it came to business and this the first time I had gotten her alone. She had been avoiding me on intimate levels since I seen her at the hospital when Kia was admitted.

"Don't tell me no Amber," I breathed in her ear and begin to smell her scent that got me on rock hard. I lifted her leg up and made my way to her smooth kitty kat and was happy she didn't have on no panties. She was wet just like I liked her. I kissed her deeply and she never even stopped me. I swiftly at that point picked her up as she grabbed my face with both of her hands deeply kissing me. I walked her over to the kitchen area that blocked us from being in Maliyah's view. I planted her ass on the countertop, and we began to passionately kiss. Reaching her neck, I sucked on it for dear life. She moaned sensually, which made me ready to burst. Pulling down my basketball shorts I allowed her to slide down on my dick. We moaned in union. Damn she felt untouched and tight. I bite her neck trying not to come so fast.

"Damn baby, I missed this," I whispered in her ear and her legs began to shake. One thing I knew for sure is that Amber could not take nasty talk it always made her cum instantly. I slow stroked her trying to savor the moment. I was trying to reach her soul in every stroke. Amber's moans made my dick get to happy. I had to think of different things to not make me cum.

"Shit!" she yelped trying to hold on to me and the counter, all a while trying to take dick.

"Tell me you love me!" I kissed her feverishly.

"Hmmm shit, baby!" Amber moaned, but I knew what she was doing. Stroking her deeper again.

"Tell me you love me," and I stroked upward trying to reach her soul as her moan sounded like a pleasant high note.

"I love you," She finally admitted, sounding like the best thing I ever heard. I tried so hard, but I couldn't help it. The moment I felt her body shake and juices coat me like a waterfall, I lined her walls with my nut. Holding her tight, while she wrapped her arms around my neck holding on for dear life.

"Baby, you choking me," I told her and she loosened her grip while trying to get her breathing under control. I heard her whimpering, which made me pull her slightly away. "You crying?" I asked in confusion.

"This is just so bad. Why couldn't you just leave me alone Mack?" She whined.

"I'm sorry Amber. I miss us. A nigga lost without you," I began to stroke her again, because her walls were warm, and my dick got even stiffer while still inside.

I kissed her tears away, which only made them fall more. I sexed Amber on that counter again, hoping this would make her come home. It was like the minute we were done, Maliyah woke up just in time. My baby for once was not being no hater. I convinced Amber to not leave and just stay with us for the day. She was trying so hard to leave but after I fed Maliyah and put her in the room to watch JoJo on YouTube, sis wasn't moving until she needed food. I got Amber in that room and laid her ass out. She was done for, knocked out sleeping after the rounds I put in to keep her around me. I showered and found Maliyah in the room playing with her toys without a care in the world. I got her stuff together because I knew her mom was on the way to get her. As if on cue, I heard the knock at the door. Grabbing all Maliyah's stuff that she came with and picking her up as well, I walked to the door and opened it. I saw an annoyed Tina.

"I thought we agreed to not have her around our kids," Tina instantly started snapping.

"Man, c'mon with that shit. You know eventually we gon have peoples and Amber is my fiancé," I expressed.

"Nigga, I don't give a fuck! You got to be the dumbest nigga there is because word around town she fuckin on Troy, but you round here still being dumb for the bitch that broke us up," she bitterly said.

"Tina, I don't care what the streets say. She's here with me now, so take our daughter home, because it's getting late and cool out this fucking door," I barked handing her the baby bag and Maliyah. She was about to say something else, but I slammed the door in her face and locked it. I didn't care what no one said, Amber was with a nigga now and I was determined more than ever to keep her. We both did fucked up shit to each other, and it didn't mean we were any less than the other. I was just hoping she was still willing to work it out, because these days bitches were worse than niggas and would say anything to make a nigga shut up. Feeling the weight of what Tina said I became curious. I walked over to Amber's bag on the counter. I dug in it for the phone. Looking at it for a few moments I contemplated on opening it, but as soon as I put it down the phone began to ring. Seeing a picture of Amber and the nigga Troy hugged up like a couple made me want to break her phone into pieces.

"Yo," I found myself answering Amber's phone. I went against everything stood for right now, but I was pissed. The chuckle that came from the nigga voice made me want to come at him again.

"Damn. Nigga you couldn't just let her answer phone. That pic hurt your pride hunh?" Troy taunted me.

"Nigga, I got some more bullets, but you won't live next time around, so I would shut all that shit talking down my nigga," I snapped.

"Man, unlike you, I don't have to do all that. Just let her know I'm waiting on her," he laughed before hanging up. That shit had me so hot I marched my ass to the damn room and snatched naked ass Amber the fuck up. I mean we weren't together, but this Troy nigga needed to go.

"What the fuck! Mack let me go what's your problem?" she screamed.

"So, you fucking that nigga?" I snapped trying to choke the sense back into her ass.

"Mack please!" she clawed at my hands. I slammed her body back on the bed and tried my best to control my anger. Amber jumped up and far away from me scared as hell.

"Amber, are you fucking this nigga?" I asked calmly this time. I needed to be rational. I was going off impulse.

"Mack you got to stop! This is insane. I knew it was a mistake staying here and doing this," She cried trying to find her clothes around the room.

"Amber, you not leaving this house to go lay up with that nigga!" I barked and she jumped.

"Nigga, you got a lot of fucking balls!" Amber's scared face went to disgust. I watched her quickly put on her clothes, and head to grab her purse from out of the kitchen.

"Amber you leave this house I'm cutting your ass off!" I threatened and she laughed in my face.

"Nigga, please you ain't dumb nor crazy. I tried to be cool about shit, but I dictate how I want to live my life dealing with a nigga who got two kids from the same woman," she wiped her eyes as she tried to stand tall, but I knew her all too well. I walked forward grabbing her as she fell into my arms and broke down. It's crazy how much we needed each other. She was the one that caused half this shit, but I definitely didn't have to do her the way I did with Tina. I wished I could make Tina get rid of the baby, but I knew the spite wouldn't allow her too.

HOME SWEET HOME

Kia

It was finally time for me to go home I was out my first trimester and close to my third trimester at twenty-four weeks. I spent about two months in the hospital and now I was free. I was finally able to keep solid foods down and gain proper weight. I could finally see my stomach protruding. My cousins were super excited because they were dead set on having a gender reveal and baby shower. They wanted a Thanksgiving reveal and a winter wonderland shower. I Honestly just wanted to go home. I had to admit between Yams and Renzo I was worn out. It was like once one left the other one came. I swear I was happy that they never even so much as ran into each other at the hospital. Renzo was adamant about bringing me home, but I told him no. I never told him why, but I had Yams coming to bring me home. I sat on the edge of the hospital bed finishing up my packing. Yams walked in with a bouquet of flowers. That made my heart smiled. The yellow tulips were everything.

"You know this baby got me soft. Oh my God, this is so sweet of you," I smiled as my eyes watered. This nigga was laying it on thick. He was always buying me flowers or doing something super sweet. He would write me love notes and leave them while I slept and buy me random gifts.

"Anything for you beautiful," He said planting a kiss on my forehead. The nurse walked in and her face went from pleasant to confusion and shock.

"Um, Ms. Gray these are your discharge papers," she said eyeing Yams suspiciously, which was low key annoying. "I forgot to get you something the doctor prescribed just in case you get nauseas. I'll be right back." She said and left back out.

"Yams, you know her?" I asked him, turning around slightly annoyed. I noticed he was turned around getting my bag. I almost felt like he was hiding or something.

"Naw, I don't know her, why?" he asked facing me.

"She looked shocked or almost confused when she saw your face. You sure you don't know her?" I asked him again.

"Naw, maybe she thought she knew me," he shrugged. I eyed him suspiciously because one thing for sure my intuition never lied. Let me find out he was fucking my nurse. He never had issues until he had a Kia issue. The nurse finally came back in, and she handed me the script. I watched her but this time her demeanor changed.

"Well, Kia we will see you back when it's time to deliver. We enjoyed your presence on this floor." She smiled, but for some reason, I felt like she wanted to tell me something so bad.

"Maybe when I get situated, I can bring you lunch one day," I told her as she walked us out. I could tell Yams was fidgeting and uncomfortable, because he was trying to rush us the way he was speed walking.

"Yes, that would be nice, but I better hurry because he about to leave you," she chuckled. I joined in, but something was definitely off with this nigga. The minute we got in the car, I had to speak my mind. One thing my grandma always told me was to speak my mind no matter how much it may hurt.

"Yams, what is that all about?" I asked him.

"What you talkin about?" he looked dumb founded. I took a deep breath.

"Listen, I played games all my life and I know when someone is playing games with me. That girl either know you or seen you somewhere. She looked confused as hell. So what the hell you have going on that you were hiding?" I stated. He looked at me with that infectiousness smile.

"Listen, if there is anything I need to let you know, I will tell you. I promise. Just relax and don't worry yourself over nothing," he kissed the back of my hand. I wasn't satisfied with his answer, but I promised myself I would pay more attention to the nigga, because niggas lie every day.

We drove the rest of the way home in silence. Pulling up in the driveway I was so happy to finally be home. I opened the door ready to see my bed. I had my curly coils down. I had on a fitted dress that came to my knees. My belly was protruding now, and I was getting heavy again in my legs, thighs and ass. I think at this point I was so happy I could keep foods down, I wanted to eat everything I could get my hands on at this point. I was so excited to get in the house I was fumbling with my keys. Once I got the door open.

"Surprise!" Everyone screamed I was so in shock, I just stood there. Yams walked up behind me and smiled. I looked at some of my family and couldn't believe it. The one that shocked me the most was the women who birthed me. Standing next to Renzo. I was so emotional I forgot I had Yams with me. My cousins rushed me excitedly.

"OMG girl!" Amber pulled me away from Yams as he brought in all my stuff.

"Why the fuck is Renzo here?" I asked.

"Well you were supposed to go home with him, but as usual you so stubborn, but you good. I talked to him and he said he will be civil." Heaven said.

"Civil? Bitch he lied to you," I expressed in panic.

"I tried to tell Heaven. He's about to embarrass Yams," Amber said not giving a fuck about what happened.

"Girl I doubt it. Renzo met his match when it came to Yams, but c'mon let's go speak to our family," Heaven said pulling me again.

"Kia, I'm so glad you're ok. I been praying for you since Amber told us what happened," My auntie Sheila said who is Ambers mom.

"Thanks auntie," I hugged her.

"Girl now don't let yo mama stress you with her shit, but Renzo got her here," Sheila began talking. One thing for sure my auntie knew everything even if you didn't tell her yourself. I nodded my head as she went on and on about how my mama wasn't no good.

"Sheila you going to real life talk about me as if I'm not in this room. Let me talk to my daughter," Ava cut her off. I was relieved because auntie could talk, but I wasn't interested honestly in what my mother had to say.

"Girl bye, you haven't spoken to this baby in years," auntie Sheila scoffed and walked off. I notice Yams staring at me and he winked, while he chatted with some of my daddy's side of my family. I smiled and he looked away and I noticed Renzo walk up behind my mother.

"So that's why you didn't want me to get you? Your other nigga came and got you," he mocked.

"Renzo why didn't you bring Nadia? Or she don't know we having a baby?" I asked and he glared at me.

"Wait I thought y'all two were together," Ava asked, and I rolled my eyes.

"How much he paid you to be here?" I asked Ava. I was annoyed with her already.

"I didn't pay her shit. She came on her own. I told her what was up, and she got happy cause your ass pregnant," he shrugged. I couldn't believe it because she never cared about me so why my unborn.

"Listen, Kia I know I haven't been a good mother but it's hard to even look at you sometimes," her eyes watered. "Your daddy was everything and you was everything to him and the fact I couldn't give you him, I just could never face you," she touched my hand and I looked at her as if she had a disease.

"I hear you Ava, but please don't touch me," I simply said and walked off leaving the two people I couldn't stand the most together.

I mingled with my family and ate. I was happy to see my aunts, uncles, and cousins. It took me back to being at my grandma's house and she would have all the holiday dinners at her house. I loved the holidays because of her. I was happy that Amber and Heaven decorated the house in a fall décor just in time for Thanksgiving. It was good to be around all my family as we planned to for Thanksgiving, which according to Amber and Heaven that will be my gender reveal and it would be big. I sat eating sweet potato pie, with a smile until I felt a presence next to me. Looking at Renzo I rolled my eyes.

"Man, you love me then hate me Kia. What's up with that?" Renzo sat next to me.

"Renzo, I realized you're just my baby daddy. Out of all the stress and shit you put me through, that's all we will ever be, so I'm sorry if one minute I like you and the next minute I'm angry with you. Like you fucking the plug, you back doored me on my money, I can't even fuck with you," I expressed. I was about to get up, but Yams came up.

"You good baby?" Yams purposely said the last part. This nigga wanted to get shit poppin.

"Nigga, she good," Renzo stayed. I knew he had enough of Yams. He been playing nice for a while, but I knew he was about to snap because he been playing patient for a while.

"Nigga we got pressure because I asked her not you," Yams retorted.

"Nigga she talking to me. The nigga who put a baby in her," his rude ass said.

"Oh, you sure about that," he chuckled and just that quick the party was over, and shit got crazy. The way Renzo jumped on Yams, I knew if we didn't stop him, he was going to kill him. Everyone tried to separate the two. I was in the middle yelling and holding my stomach with tears. This was too much. For the life of me I couldn't understand the logic behind Yams words. This nigga was tripping.

"I want y'all two out my shit now!" I screamed, as my chest heaved up and down. I couldn't believe the shit that went on. The minute the niggas got outside; it started all over again. They were going blow for blow. I noticed Chase, Ricardo and Mack pull up, but they tried their best to pry them apart. I was praying that this shit didn't go any further because I couldn't handle something else bad happening. I pushed through everyone to get outside. Yams was bloodied up. I went by his side as he chuckled lightly.

"Oh, nigga you thought you got one up on me hunh?" I pulled Yams, with the help of my mom, Amber, and Heaven. I watched as Renzo tried to fight to get to Yams again. I noticed Yams was taunting him winking and shit. I want to punch his ass in the eye. I didn't like this vindictive side of him. Once we were able to get him inside, Heaven got everyone to leave. My aunts and mom stayed still talking about the situation. I was cleaning Yams up in the room.

"What was that Yams?" I calmly asked.

"Kia, yo BD feel like he entitled, is he?" He snapped on me. I was about to go off because one thing I didn't deal with is a nigga talking crazy to me.

"Yams, y'all both were out of line, but let's be clear. Watch your tone with me or you gon get what Renzo gets when I lose my fucking cool." I got up throwing the damn gauze at him. I stormed out of my room and down the hall. When I made it to the living area, I watched as my aunts and mama clean up the mess the men made. I walked outside to see Ricardo, Heaven and Chase talking.

"Yo, boss lady. What you doing to my nigga," Chase was ready to be funny.

"I didn't do nothing. He needs to just chill. He always wants to be on damn ten," I was annoyed.

"Black people always tearin' shit up," Chase continued his foolishness.

"Chase shut up!" I snapped.

"Well, I didn't do it is all I'm gon say," he threw his hands up.

"Where is he?" I asked knowing they had to drive the nigga away.

"Man, Mack had to drive that nigga away. You lucky the hammer was in the car because he was about to put a bullet in ol boy," Ricardo responded.

"I ain't gon lie, ol boy got bitch in him. Like the nigga tweakin with the comments he making." Chase said but I already felt the same way. Yams was becoming territorial and trying his best to get under the Renzo's skin.

"They competing with hot pussy over here," Heaven said making Chase fall out in laughter.

"They say good pussy make these niggas bitches," Chase continued. I was done listening to them. This had been one fucked up day.

"Chase I'm two seconds from decking your ass!" I frowned my face.

"That's my cue to go. Lets ride Ricardo," Chase quickly got up ready to leave. He knew when I was ready, I would whoop me a nigga's ass if I needed too.

"Listen sis, I love you, but y'all two need to figure this shit out, because shit about to get real hectic and ain't nothing good coming from fucking with people hearts. That nigga in yo house is on a mission. Mark my words. Shit ain't what it seems," Ricardo dropped some wisdom on me before he gave me a hug goodbye. I watched him grab Heaven and whisper something in her ear that made her turn beet red with joy. Honestly, I thought they were cute together. He would definitely keep her in line.

Heaven and I walked back inside the house, and Yams was coming out of the room on the phone I watched him walk in my direction and I could tell by his demeanor he did not look happy at all. I admired his tall physique and how his chocolate smooth skin didn't hold one bruise from the fight. The nosebleed seems to have stopped. Before he made it directly in front of me within arm's reach, he disconnected the line. I stared up at the handsome man and realized that Yams was feeling me way more than I thought.

"Shit about to get hectic Kia," he said, letting me know he was on some drill type shit.

"Why can't y'all both just chill?" I began to get upset all over again.

"You're the reason the shit is like this," He frowned.

"Excuse me?" I rolled me neck and took a step back.

"Kia, you can't let go of him. You constantly have this nigga around even after I told you and showed you, I got you! I swear you only having the nigga baby is because you still want apart of him. Matter of fact, holla at a nigga when this situation is dead, because you getting a nigga salty as fuck," I watched Yams walk out the door, and even though my feelings were hurt, I think it was the best thing for the both of us at the moment. Heaven walked next to me putting her arm around me to comfort me. *What a first day out this was!* I said to myself. As I leaned on my cousins shoulder.

HELL HAS NO FURY LIKE A
WOMAN SCORNED

Nadia

Renzo had been on his best behavior these days. He had been very attentive to my needs. He had become a better leader for his team, allowing them to handle things on their own when he was not around. He held his occasional meetings just so that his workers knew he was still around. Money was flowing better than before, so I knew my plan would work out in my best interest. Renzo was massaging my feet allowing me to relax. Ever since my uncle been in the hospital, I had not been able to rest. Even though money was still being made, you could tell the movement was slow, since everything had to be run by Lolita. I was lowkey mad that he left everything for her to delegate, which meant I probably wasn't going to be able to get a dime or help the way I knew how.

"Babe let's do a baecation," I suggested. He looked at me with those dreamy low eyes that let me know he was high as hell.

"Damn, sounds good. Where you want to go?" he asked, while he continued to work his fingers into my feet, massaging them.

"Well, I was thinking, like Cuba or Turks. Just something with a beach and water." I said excitedly.

"We can decide later on the date and stuff. Maybe next year or something," he said making me instantly annoyed.

"Why we got to wait so long? I want to go this weekend," I stated, and he looked at me like I was crazy.

"Look, I still got shit to handle here. Why the hell would we go so soon? I already got beef wit yo guy Yams and I just had to move my trap. As well as trying to make sure I move these products as fast as I get them. Shit is a damn hassle by itself. Who gon run the shit without me," He complained and all I heard was excuses.

"So, what is Mack for?" I asked curiously. He needed to let these niggas step up or he would always do all the damn work. Even though he was moving in the right direction, he had his moments where he babied his workers.

"Mack and I do this shit together and on some real shit, the way I run my shit is how I run my shit. Stop telling a nigga what to do. You always doing the most and not accepting the answers I give," He stated without a care in the world. Snatching my leg back.

"For some reason, I feel like you trying to do other shit," I folded my arms and pouted my lips. I didn't care that I look like a little girl at this point. I needed things to go my way.

"Nadia, we just came back from a damn month long vacation. Like what's up with you? I give you all the time in the world and some time the shit is never enough for you," He was becoming aggravated, but I didn't care. One thing about me I always get what I want.

"Does it matter? You must got you someone else you need to stay in town for," I pulled the cheating card, but that only made him madder.

"Nadia, I'm going to go. I need a break from you." He got up and headed for the bedroom. I followed behind him in a rush because I really didn't want him to go.

"Baby," I pulled his arm, but he yanked it away.

"No, you need to stop this crazy shit," he began putting his phones and keys in his pockets.

"Renzo, you leave out that door and we going to have a serious problem!" I demanded. He looked at me shaking his head.

"Or what? You going to beat my ass," he laughed.

"No, but I will make you cry," I said and made my way back to the couch. Renzo walked back out in the living room and without another word he walked out the door.

I wasn't into playing games with these niggas, but I learned that Renzo was the type to do his own thing and deal with the consequences later. Once Renzo was gone, I needed to make a few calls. The first one was to Yams because I needed to know what was really going on. Even though Renzo hasn't been out of my sight lately, I felt like something was off. I couldn't put my hand on what it was, but I knew it was something that had him low-key distracted. I called Yams, but he didn't answer me. I sent him a message for us to meet and he responded agreeing. I got up and pulled my hair in a neat ponytail. I then threw on a track suit and sneakers. I wanted to be comfortable, plus the wind was really blowing in Miami. It's crazy how one minute it could be hot and the next minute it's cool outside with wind. I grabbed my keys off the counter along with my purse and made my way to the meet up spot. As I quickly drove in and out of traffic, it only took me like fifteen minutes to make it to the location. I wanted us to meet at behind some abandoned buildings deep in Miami. Parking, I sat and patiently waited for him to show up. After about thirty minutes of waiting he pulled up. Putting my gun in the small of my back I hopped out of the car and walked towards him. I had to admit when Yams got out the car, he was looking damn good, with the wind blowing so strong I got a whiff of his cologne. He stood tall and his swag and demeanor always demanded attention. He screamed boss, but to me Renzo yelled gGangsta and to me that was better because that meant he will always be on go.

"So, what's the 911 emergency? A nigga got shit to handle," he said smoothly. Even though most would choose Yams over Renzo, Renzo would always be the better pick in my opinion.

"I need to know what is going on with Renzo and Kia," I asked. He looked at me with the same cold stare.

"Nothing, really. The nigga and I done had some words, but it ain't shit I can't handle. I do think you to keep your nigga on a leash." He truthfully told me.

"What are you talking about? I made the nigga disappear for a month straight," I was confused because I know I have been keeping a close eye on Renzo.

"Well, Nadia you ain't watching the nigga good enough. The nigga been seeing Kia constantly since you came back in town, and I can honestly see him wearing Kia down, and honestly I been trying not to kill ol' boy because of you," he truthfully told me. Him and Renzo's beef was getting deeper and deeper. I already let Yams know that he was not to kill him, even if he wanted too.

"Yams, if anyone killing anybody it's me and you must be falling for Kia, because you definitely want to keep her ass alive. So, what you plan on doing about the pregnant wife?" I was curious at this point.

"You call the shots on this situation for now, but let me tell you something, while you it back and delegating, I get my hands dirty. I told you once and I'm going to tell you again. This ain't the movies and you ain;t the only person that got dope. I would rather pay the extra then to deal wit yo ass anymore. I will tell Kia in my own time, but until then put yo boy on a leash or I'm laying his ass out. I'm not playing fair no more. I been letting dude slide too many times," he calmly expressed. This is what I mean about Yams. He wasn't a hot head. He was strategic.

"Yams do what I say. I hate to be crossed or I promise when I get mad, I'm snatching everyone up out of life." I stated.

"Shit word on the street is you and Renzo about to lose anyway. Since Vinny is down bad, I wonder who the business would go to. You know the nigga loved Kia especially Lolita." He sneered and walked away.

The little meeting didn't go as planned and now my whole head was fucked up and lost. I needed to go see my uncle, but Lolita had him on a careful watch. I watched Yams get in the car and drive away. The wheels in my head began to turn because I needed to gain control of things. I didn't work hard to lose to some bitch out the hood. I walked away headed back to the car. It was time to really figure out my next move, and for some reason

I felt like Renzo was hiding some shit. Which, I was definitely about to find out about it. My phone rang taking me out of my thoughts. Seeing it was Kaylee I answered the phone, hoping it was nothing major.

"Hello, boss lady. I know you didn't want to be bothered, but I need you to come in for a few minutes. My mother called..." I cut Kaylee off.

"I understand, I'm on the way," I assured her. Kaylee's mom was very sick, and she was the only person that could care for her. Sometimes she had to run out to the nursing home for different things to help them with, so I never even bothered her on it, because she would always come back to work afterwards. I would have normally gone home and changed, but since I was out, I just went to the office. I walked in and it was pleasant to see clients at almost everyone's desk. I quickly walked around greeting everyone. I made it to Kaylee's desk, and she had worried lines across her forehead.

"I'm so sorry about this, but I will be back in an hour," she confirmed rushing past me and out the door. I set her phone to transfer the calls to my desk. I then went into the room I created as a kitchen and lounge for breaks or just peace and quiet. I noticed Heaven was sitting on her laptop uploading pictures. The problem was walking past her the one that stood out to me was the one of Kia, with a small barely visible baby bump, and Renzo holding her the way he would hold me. I felt my temperature rise like boiling hot water. I was ready to go to war about my broken heart. This nigga played me for the last time. No amount of love will make me forgive this shit. I wasn't Kia. I real life kill behind my heart. I went against all my standards for Renzo and look how he played me.

"Hello Heaven. How are you today?" I played nice to figure out what the hell she was up to and who was Kia to her.

"Hello Nadia. I was just uploading my cousins welcome home pictures to my computer. I'm making a collage for her gender reveal. It's on Thanksgiving," she disclosed. How ironic, they were cousins. I can't believe Heaven didn't know who I was. They couldn't have been that close, but now it explains Renzo's moods, and why didn't Yams disclose this information. I had so many questions at this point and now I felt like everyone around me needed to go. The first person that was about to be taken out was Yams, because he was supposed to be providing this information to me and it seem like he was being a whole snake.

"Well, your cousin looks beautiful. How far along is she is?" I asked.

"Honestly, she is about twenty-four weeks, and we are so excited to finally do a gender reveal and baby shower," she smiled excitedly. I cringed at the thought of her enjoying being pregnant by Renzo.

"Well, that's nice. I know she is going to die when she sees everything you guys have planned," I plastered the best fake smile I could.

"Yes, it is, but let me get back to work. I have a client coming in soon." She unplugged her phone and closed the laptop and smiled before walking out of the door. Once she was gone my smile was completely gone. I paced the floor slightly frustrated trying to gather my thoughts. One thing for sure, no nigga was going to have one up on me. I took a deep breath and walked out of the breakroom and to my office. I closed the door and pulled my cell phone out and dialed the person I needed to speak with. The first thing in order was to kill Yams, and anyone affiliated with him. I was about to make these niggas feel me!

LAST DAYS

Yams

I finally left the traps and was about to head home to my wife and newborn. I was so happy to have a new baby, but I wished it was with the person I was really in love with and that was Kia. Ever since I met Kia, I been drawn to her on a different level. The things I said to her I actually meant them. She was different and the fact she wanted more out of life then what she was doing was what I loved about her. My wife just loved the hype of being with Yams not Zeke. While there was no connection there. I shared those moments with Kia. I had every intention on ending the relationship. I just was waiting on her to have the baby, and she was adjusted. I'm not going to lie it has been a struggle trying to juggle them both, but it was easy to tell my wife I was making money and always out. She never questioned me or made a noise about not giving her any attention, which made it easy for me to do. Troy and Jay expressed that I was crazy to even be fucked up with Kia, being that she had a crazy side that I never experienced. I had plans on keeping it that way, but for right now I was on a mission and that was to let my wife Karina know that I was filing a separation and then we were going to get a divorce. I needed that distraction gone to focus more on Kia. I knew if I applied the right pressure, I could make Kia fold because all she wanted was a nigga to love her properly and I was that person for her whether she knew it or not. When I brought her home from the hospital, I didn't even know there was anything going on like that, but to see that fuck nigga there, I was not leaving. He felt like he could pop in and out of her life like he wanted to. If I had a woman like Kia, I would have never left in the first place. Like she didn't know it yet, but I had got her a building where she could set up her financial services. My baby just needed a push and the right nigga to do that.

Pulling up in the driveway, the home I had in Weston, was nice. I looked at how my wife had a waterfall put in the front yard. The brown colors made the house seem warm. I got out of the whip and noticed the yard man had just cut the yard. I put my key in the door and walked inside. I could hear Karina singing to my newborn daughter. It took me back to the night she was born. I was already in the hospital and had to leave my wife's side to be there for Kia. I noticed the nurse who discharged Kia was the nurse that helped deliver Karina's baby. I knew the lady wanted to say something so bad, but I tried my best to get the hell out of dodge.

I am in love with you (In love)

You set me free

I can't do this thing called life without you

here with me

Cause I'm dangerously in love with you (In love)

I'll never leave

Just keep loving me the way I love you

loving me

She sung her heart out to the little baby in her arms who stared at her as she moved. I had to admit, we made a beautiful daughter. I walked over to them and she smiled up at me. I leaned down to kiss her forehead. My daughter was everything to me. I hated that she would not experience a two-parent household.

"What's wrong Zeke?" she asked. Not wanting to hold it off much longer, I sat next to her on the couch.

"Listen, our relationship is not working. Like we have a daughter but my only connection I feel is through her. We have been together for years and nothing has changed in our relationship. We are intimate only when need be. Other than that we lack everything that we should have." I tried to explain to her. She looked at me and she just stared blankly.

"So, who is she?" she asked, and I didn't want to even name anyone.

"Why does that matter?" I asked becoming annoyed.

"Because Zeke, I knew you been cheating. I just didn't give a damn. You chose to be intimate and share those things with someone else. You never even gave me a try to be what you wanted because you wanted it in someone else. You assumed I wanted to sit home alone, but that's far from the truth. Hmph, I can't believe I ever loved someone like you."

"And what's that supposed to mean?" I began to get upset.

"Tone yourself down because our baby is in my arms. I may not be the girl you want, but I'm still your wife! Respect me! I think you should leave because you're right, enough is enough," she was firm, and continued to coddle our daughter.

I was a little thrown off, because she was so calm. I felt like she knew something I didn't. I walked upstairs and began packing my stuff to leave the house. I had already got me a little spot, so it was nothing to move. Once I finished gathering what I needed I walked downstairs, and noticed Karina was gone from out of the living room. I had placed my things at the door and was ready to say my goodbyes. I walked in the kitchen and noticed she had dinner laid out with candles. That looked to be blown out. Damn, I felt slightly bad because she was trying while I created a whole relationship with someone else.

"Damn, this was all for me?" I stupidly asked.

"Yea, but our relationship ran its course remember?" I could see her eyes water. I now felt bad that I decided to choose a woman over my family, that could never choose me, but I felt like Kia was my soul.

"You allowed me to be with you for years, knowing you didn't love me the way you should. You didn't have the decency to even try. I spent all this time alone because you said you was building something for us so you could stop, but instead you fell in love with another woman." She expressed shaking her head at me in disbelief. Karina was beautiful, and at times I didn't know what would make me want to leave her. I was about to say something, but she cut me off immediately.

"Honestly, I don't want to hear your excuses or apologies. Just tell me this, when did you know that you were done?" she decided to ask, and even though I felt like it was weird I still answered her.

"I want to say three to four months now," I guessed. She shook her hair more.

"Fuck you and everything you stand on. That's why you left the hospital during the delivery hunh?" She pointed her finger at me. I didn't want to answer her, and I was afraid she might get rowdy, because she was doing more than I ever seen her do the whole relationship.

"For what it's worth, I'm sorry I just thought that…" the splatter of blood hitting my face cut me off. I paused and was incoherent to what I was seeing. I slide my hands across my face and then looked at the blood stains. I watched Karina fall back with our daughter in her arms. I turned around quickly and saw one of Nadia's bodyguard standing there with his arm extended and the gun pointed. I looked back down and notice the red blood that began to spill crimson red on to the pink blanket that my daughter was wrapped in. Checking both of their pulse I noticed there was none, and the bullet went through one and hit the other killing them both. My heart shattered in pieces. My very first child gone and there was nothing I could do about it. I grabbed them both and held them in my arms. For the first time in life I cried. I knew I shouldn't have turned my back on the armed security guard, but my mind was on my daughter and Karina, and I how I failed them. I played Karina and put them in harm's way. There is no way I should have ever fucked with Nadia. I heard stories of how she got down, but never really experienced them.

"I told you not to play me," Nadia's voice made my skin crawl. I got up and saw nothing, but red. I charged at her but was snatched up by two other security guards that I never even notice.

"See, I had every intention on letting you live so you could mourn your little family that you were about to leave, and have you blamed for the crime, but that was too much work, so I decided since you're so hard up, I'll break you apart limb from limb to make disposable process easy and then kill you," Her sick ass said.

I knew I was going to die a painful death, but a nigga wasn't going to bitch up now. They began to beat me up and then started to break my ankles and legs I think at some point I was already dead, because I was mentally checked out and the pain went numb. I think I was going into shock. The sound of my wrists and arms breaking would make anyone wince in pain, but me I was already dead so the grunts that were able to escape as they broke my body up as much as they could while I was alive. I heard her heels walking towards me and then the last thing I heard her say was "Shoot em". Hearing the silencer release, everything went black and my pain was no longer there. I guess I will see my baby in heaven if I make it there.

BLACK OUT

Renzo

The air was cool and windy for once in Miami it was nighttime, and it was not hot as hell outside. I was in the hood with my brother and homeboys kicking shit in Opa-locka. Opa-locka was another hood that people feared to come in, but to me it was home and will always have my heart. I mean Opa-locka was sort of big and not all of it was bad. Well to me rather. I was throwing the dice and when those dice rolled to my winning number I yelled out, while them niggas crabbed loudly, mad as hell for losing they money. Picking up my money, my phone rung.

"Hey, niggas hol up! My phone ringing!" I yelled at them to not start the next game without me. "Yo," I said into my phone.

"Renzo, I'm not feeling to well. Do you mind coming over? I have been over the toilet nonstop and I have been having nose bleeds really bad," Kia panicked.

"Ok, I got you. I'm coming, just sit tight," I told her.

I already felt bad for the situation I put us in, and the least I could do was be there for her. She was six months pregnant now and I couldn't leave her hanging because she already been through so much shit dealing with me. Ever since I tried to kill her little boyfriend that day at her welcome home party from the hospital, I have tried to keep my distance from her. That is until the nigga was found murdered in the house with a wife and child. Kia had been dependent on me ever since and I found it kind of crazy, but I didn't fault her for it. I didn't mind, but it was funny how all her cousins were team him and this nigga had a whole damn family he was hiding. I just felt bad for the daughter. That was a newborn and I didn't know what type of person just kills a baby. They are innocent. The bad part about this is, I had to keep clearing my name because word on the street me and my niggas did it, but that wasn't on us. Kia thought I did it but once she heard a little innocent baby was involved, she knew I could never. Kia's baby bump was finally showing and watching life grow in her just made me fall in love all over again.

"Ok, and Renzo thank you, and no matter what, I love you!" she said for the first time in during this whole situation. *Damn she really bending for a nigga* I thought to myself. It's been a while since Kia said those words and damn, I felt it. She didn't know but I was going to come home if she let me and I wouldn't dare stray again. I rather be with her and my child. It was the day before Thanksgiving and we were having a gender reveal with the family, something small because the baby shower was in a few weeks. Heaven and Amber had shit mapped out.

"Dum love Shawdy. I'm on my way," I told her. I hung up the phone and looked at my niggas. "Y'all I got to slide and see Kia before going home" I said to them. Everyone said their goodbyes to me. My brother Ricardo walked with me to my car.

"You think you should be risking going over to Kia's house just yet with that crazy bitch of yours going mad," Ricardo expressed. He was more worried about Nadia than I was. He was convinced that she did that shit to Yams, and I was next. He claimed Yams only had us he was beefing with and the only people able to do what she did is her, but I didn't see it that way.

"Man, she home and I'm not staying over there." I told him.

"Yea, nigga but that hoe told you if you take yo ass around her one more time she was killing you and Kia," he said worried. I don't know why I even bothered telling hm about the argument I had with Nadia. She said shit like that all the time but never act on them.

"Nigga, she crazy but she ain't that silly. Plus I got y'all to hunt that hoe down if she do," I shrugged said, but Ricardo was not feeling that shit at all.

"I mean nigga I'm gon do my part, but I think you need to play this shit safe until you got a fucking plan to leave the girl!" he expressed in all seriousness. Ricardo was a thinker and a planner.

He hated for some shit to pop off and he not be prepared for it. He did everything as such. That's why I loved him. He always had a plan for something or way out of a situation.

"Trust me bro, I'm good and you don't have to worry about shit!" I told Ricardo. He nodded his head in agreement, but I could tell from his eyes and body language he was just too unsure and not feeling my decision.

"Aiight, bro," He clapped me up and I hopped in my whip and headed to Kia's house.

While driving my phone rung seeing it was Nadia. I immediately got annoyed. I thought about not answering it, but I knew if I didn't, she would just blow me up until she got me. She had become more aggressive lately and always wanting to be around me or not too far away from me. Regretting answering the call, I press the green button on my phone.

"Yo," I said.

"You sound annoyed Renzo," she stated.

"I'm good. What's up?" I asked her.

"I think it's time you come home. It's late,"
she stated again. She was talking to me like a drill
sergeant and the shit was annoying. I was starting to
think she knew something or had a GPS on me this
point, because I knew for sure I hadn't been
followed.

"Nadia, I'm your nigga, not one of your
workers. I will come home when I'm fucking
ready!" I snapped. This girl had been crossing all
type of lines. It was all good in the beginning, but
now this shit was pure fucking hell. The line was
quiet for a few seconds, which felt like she was
really listening to the background.

"Where are you going?" she finally asked.

"To my brother's house. Is that ok with
you?" I sarcastically asked.

"No, but please don't be long," she advised,
and I pulled the phone away from my ear and
couldn't believe the shit she just said.

"Bit…!" I paused catching myself and
groaned in annoyance. "Don't wait up for me, I'll
see you when I get there!" I snapped and before I

could hang up, I heard her say she was sorry, but it was too late she already made me mad, I hung up the phone and continued my drive to Kia.

Finally, pulling up I got a phone call from my Ricardo. We chopped it up and of course he warned me again about Nadia. It's like he was really worried, and I felt like maybe he knew something and wasn't telling me. I was the only one that wasn't fearful when it came to her. I felt like I knew her better than anyone, but of course that is always not the case either. Walking up to the front door, I rang the doorbell. A nigga like me needed to get a key because she took forever sometimes to come to the door. I knew she would give me a hard time, but some needed finessing I knew I could work to getting the key to her place. After about two minutes, Kia opened the door moving back with one of my t-shirts on and some cotton shorts that looked like panties. She let me walk in and I closed the door behind me, making sure to lock it.

"I hope you checked the peep hole before you opened this door with your ass cheeks hanging out," I complained at the sight before me.

"Nigga, you are not my man anymore. We just sharing a child that's all!" she sassed, while walking further into the house and into the kitchen. I followed behind her. She opened the fridge and grabbed some water.

"What's wrong though?" I asked her. I looked her over and notice she looked slightly pale, and her lips looked dry and her eyes were glossy.

"I'm unsure, I have been throwing up nonstop and I had a fever earlier, but I broke it, but the crazy part is I don't have a cold," she said. She took small sips of water and went to lay on the couch. I followed and took my shoes off so I could lay with her on the couch. Her pregnancy has been so complicated. I kind of wish I just let her get rid of the baby.

We laid down on the couch and I held her in my arms and began to rub her baby bump. I sat there reflecting, while she watched the TV. I felt so guilty for putting her in a fucked-up situation, because had I just left her alone to heal or just stopped calling and texting, shit, I should have stopped showing up on her doorstep pissy ass drunk or simply just left Sashay's ass alone, then maybe we wouldn't have been in this fucked up situation. Kia had my whole heart and no matter what I did, I just couldn't shake her, and now we are bringing a child in the world. We laid there for a few minutes when she jumped up running to the bathroom. I followed behind her and held her hair back while she emptied her stomach, but when she started throwing up blood she began to panic and so did I. Trying not to alert her more, I tried my best to soothe her so we could get ready to go to the hospital. Once she was done emptying her stomach, she began crying as I wiped her mouth and tears.

"C'mon Kia, I need you to be strong. You gon be aight shawdy. Get yourself together and let's go. I will be waiting in the car." I told her. She nodded her head in agreement.

I left out the bathroom and put on my shoes. I checked my pockets for my phone to make sure it didn't fall out when I was laying on the couch. I opened the door and walked out in the night air. Walking towards my car that was parked on the side of the sidewalk. I hit the button and was reaching for the door handle. Feeling a sharp pain hit my head and another blow to the side of my face, I fell back, and everything went black.

*****

Feeling my head thumping in excruciating pain, I tried to move my hands to my head and realized they were tied behind my back. Feeling of nervousness came over me as I began to shake and move in the chair. I then realized my feet was tied to the chair as well. Opening my eyes all I saw was darkness. I swear it was so dark I almost thought I was blind. I sat in the darkness listening, trying to see if I could hear any familiar sounds like cars on the outside but it was complete silence. At this point I had to be in a sound-proof room. I was mad at myself for not paying attention to my surroundings, and now I was filled with worry. All I could think about was Kia and if she was ok? I wanted to know if she got to escape. Or did she ever come outside? Or if she was here hurt with me? My thoughts were interrupted by the sound of a latch being released and a door opening. I heard feet approaching me. Finally, a light was turned on and my eyes began to adjust. Looking before me, I was confused but then it all made sense. Looking at me with anger I knew I was going to either die or have to figure out a way out of this situation.

"What did you do with Kia?" I asked. The laugh that came behind it gave me the chills.

"When you the plug, you don't explain shit!" Cocking the gun back and aiming it at me, I knew I was going to die and there wasn't shit I could do about it. Hanging my head low, I played the past year in my head as I began to fill with regret. I just knew shit couldn't get worst, then what I went through earlier this year but hear I am staring death in the face.

"Boom!"

TO BE CONTINUED...

THANK YOU!

I want to take the time out to thank you all so much for reading Part 2 to A Boss'd Up Holiday with The Plug series! I hope you enjoyed part two and it gave you a mixture of feelings. I want to tell you all I appreciate you for taking the time to read Part 2 and Part 3 will be coming real soon!

Let's get connected! Follow me on:

Facebook: Authoress Lexi-B

Instagram: Lexib_Authoress

Made in the USA
Monee, IL
23 July 2021

74190172R00164